F. R. McClintock

Holidays in Spain

Being Some account of two tours in that country in the autumns of 1880 and 1881

F. R. McClintock

Holidays in Spain
Being Some account of two tours in that country in the autumns of 1880 and 1881

ISBN/EAN: 9783337189730

Printed in Europe, USA, Canada, Australia, Japan

Cover: Foto ©Andreas Hilbeck / pixelio.de

More available books at **www.hansebooks.com**

HOLIDAYS IN SPAIN;

BEING

SOME ACCOUNT OF TWO TOURS IN THAT COUNTRY

IN THE AUTUMNS OF 1880 AND 1881.

BY

F. R. McCLINTOCK.

"Al cielo de España voy."—*Lope de Vega.*

LONDON:

EDWARD STANFORD, 55, CHARING CROSS, S.W.

1882.

PREFACE.

THE following pages *grew* out of some notes taken during two tours in Spain in the autumns of 1880 and 1881; and as the perusal of what I had set down had proved of some interest to a few of my own immediate friends, I ventured to think that it might perhaps be made acceptable to a wider circle of readers. For this purpose I took seriously in hand the always agreeable task of revising, pruning, and recasting what I had written; and I now venture to submit my notes, in the shape they have finally assumed, to the tender mercies of an indulgent public.

Considering the romantic interest of the history of Spain, the varied character of its scenery and antiquities, and the genial nature and healthiness of its climate, especially in the southern provinces, it is somewhat astonishing that it is not oftener visited, and more written about. People rush in flocks to Italy, Switzerland, and other parts of the Continent, and read books about the places where they have been or intend to go. But Spain has been comparatively neglected by the British traveller. There is no conceivable reason for this, except, I suppose, that it has not yet become the *fashion* to go there. There are railways now to almost all the principal towns, and the accommodation, as a rule, leaves little to be desired. The hotels will certainly compare favourably with English, if not with French and German hotels. Indeed, so easy has travelling now become, that adventures are only to be found with difficulty in remote and inaccessible places.

In the introduction to his charming 'Tales of the Alhambra,' Mr. Washington Irving gives a graphic account of his journey from Seville to Granada in the spring of 1829. The roads at that time were little better than mere mule-paths, and were frequently beset by robbers. The most valuable part of the traveller's luggage had to be forwarded by the *arrieros* or carriers, while he merely retained clothing and necessaries for the journey and money for the expenses of · the road.

Stout steeds had to be provided, and a guard engaged, who was armed with a formidable *trabuco* or blunderbuss, to defend the party from *rateros* or footpads. The noontide repasts were made on the greensward by the side of brooks or fountains under shady trees; and the nights were passed in *posadas* in little towns among the mountains, and suppers were eaten to the notes of a guitar and the click of castañets, wielded by bright-eyed Andalusian maidens.

But now, whether for better or for worse, " the spirit of the age " has changed all that. Instead of an adventurous ride across lonely mountains, you lounge luxuriously in a comfortable first-class railway carriage. Instead of sending your luggage forward by the *arrieros*, you unromantically register it at Seville in the morning, and you do not see it again until it is safely deposited the same evening in your room at your hotel at Granada. Instead of " noontide repasts under groves of olive trees on the borders of rivulets," you now sit down to a well-served and substantial meal at the buffet at the Bobadilla railway station. The romance of the thing has fled;

but it must be owned that safety, combined with a saving in time and expense, is effected. The railways and their accompaniments have not obliterated the treasures of the past in the country, whether Punic, Roman, Arabian, or Christian, but have only made them more accessible. The bright blue sky and the transparent atmosphere have not yet been perceptibly obscured by smoke from locomotives, nor have the native dignity and courtesy of manner, for which Spaniards have always been so remarkable, as yet disappeared under the influence of the modern spirit. So civilisation is not so baneful a thing after all as some enthusiasts would make it out to be.

Thus much by way of introduction. My readers (if any) will, I hope, be able to form some opinion as to whether Spain is or is not a desirable country to travel in from what is set forth in the book itself. I will, therefore, no longer detain them from a perusal of its contents.

F. R. McClintock.

12, Ebury Street, S.W.
1882.

CONTENTS.

———◆◆◆———

PAGE

CHAPTER I.

Paris — *Établissements Duval*—Bordeaux — Halévy's *Les Mousquetaires de la Reine* — Bayonne — Burgos — Cathedral — Beggars — *Plaza Mayor* — *Cartuja de Miraflores* — *Arco de Santa Maria* — *Palacios* 1

CHAPTER II.

Madrid—Picture Gallery—a rainy Bull-fight—a Protestant Service 18

CHAPTER III.

Toledo — Cathedral — Mozarabic Chapel — *San Juan de los Reyes* — *Baños de la Cava* — Toledan Jews — Gates .. 32

CHAPTER IV.

Cordova — Mosque — at the Club — *Patios* 50

CHAPTER V.

Seville — Murillo — Cathedral — Alcazar and Gardens — *Torre del Oro* — Promenades 63

CHAPTER VI.

Granada — Cathedral — Alhambra — *Generalife* — a *Gitano* 75

CHAPTER VII.

A Journey by Diligence — Jaen — Madrid 91

PAGE

CHAPTER VIII.

Alcalá — Ximenes — Guadalajara — Sigüenza — Calatayud — Arragonese Costume — Zaragoza — Cathedral — *Torre Nueva* — Market-place — a *Baile Nacional* 98

CHAPTER IX.

Avignon — Pont du Gard—Nimes — Montpellier — Picture Gallery — Perpignan — Gerona — Hostalrich — Barcelona —Cathedral—*Puente del Diablo*—Tarragona—Cathedral — Cloisters — *San Pablo* 109

CHAPTER X.

Valencia—*Mercado*—*Lonja de Seda*—Cathedral—Museum Gates — Walls — Promenades — Saguntum — Theatre — *Castillo* 124

CHAPTER XI.

Madrid—*Academia de San Fernando*—Toledo—A Proud Castilian — *Cristo de la Luz* — *Casa de Mesa* — Taller del Moro — *San Pedro Martir* — San Tome — *Palacio de Galiana* 138

CHAPTER XII.

San Sebastian — *Monte Orgullo* — Fontarabia 149

CHAPTER XIII.

Conclusion — Travelling — Railways — Hotels — Cookery — Cafés — Brigands — Police — Irrigation — Watchmen —The Language — Literature, &c., &c. 156

SUMMARY OF THE PRINCIPAL EVENTS IN SPANISH HISTORY 188

LIST OF THE PRINCIPAL OBJECTS OF INTEREST IN TOLEDO 193

A SPECIMEN OF BULL-RING SLANG 195

HOLIDAYS IN SPAIN.

CHAPTER I.

PARIS, BORDEAUX, BAYONNE, BURGOS.

I HAD long been possessed with an ardent desire to visit Spain, and to see with my own eyes the country in which are laid the scenes of the adventures of the sprightly Gil Blas, and the illustrious knight, Don Quixote de la Mancha.

It does not of course follow that desires, however legitimate, invariably attain their fulfilment. An opportunity, however, at last presented itself; so, like Roderick Random, on his voyage to "New Spain," I procured "a Spanish grammar, dictionary, and some other books," and set to work to learn as much as I could of the language before starting on my travels.

We (for I was not doomed to travel in

B

solitude) had at first thought of going by
P. and O. boat to Gibraltar, and working our
way upwards from there. But the steamers
being all crowded at this time of year with
people going out to India, we found it impossible to engage what we wanted in the way
of berths. Besides, the prospect of a number
of women and children, tumbling about in
all directions, in the event of the voyage
proving unfavourable, was not an agreeable one to look forward to. The weather,
moreover, which had been beautiful for some
time, now changed very much for the worse,
and we were treated to fog, rain, and cold,
with a good deal of wind at intervals. We
thought it better, therefore, all things considered, to abandon our original intention of
entering the land of chivalry and romance by
way of the sea, and we finally decided to go
by Dover and Calais to Paris, and so on by
the usual route down to Bordeaux, Bayonne,
and Irun.

We left London on Wednesday the 6th
of October, by the evening express from
Victoria. Our start was made in the most
miserable and depressing weather imaginable,

and the prospect of a rough passage, although it was only to be a short one, caused our spirits to droop considerably. I must own that I felt the more uncomfortable of the two. Only lunatics, I thought, would dream of leaving a comfortable home, and a warm bed, in order to endure the miseries of a journey by sea and land in such weather, and at night too. However we got off notwithstanding, and were agreeably surprised, on reaching Dover, to find that the sea was rather inclined to be smooth than rough. We had an excellent passage across, and arrived in Paris in good time, without more than the usual discomfort of a night journey. But in spite of the favourable passage, some of our fellow-passengers nevertheless contrived to be ill. I did not, however, see any one ill *before* the boat started, as I once knew to be the case on coming from Boulogne to Folkestone. On that occasion, if I remember rightly, the culprit, a lady, had provided herself with a life-belt, which she wore round her waist all the way to Charing Cross. The life-belt proved to be of little use, however, as the sea was as calm as a duck-pond.

In Paris we took up our abode at the Hôtel de Calais, in the Rue Neuve des Capucines, a quiet, comfortable, and reasonable place. We only took our morning coffee, &c., there, and breakfasted and dined at those admirable institutions, the *Établissements Duval*, or *de Bouillon*, where the best of everything in the plain French style is to be had at the lowest possible cost.

I cannot help, in passing, expressing some astonishment at the very few English to be seen patronising these excellent establishments. Most of those of my countrymen whom I have spoken to on the subject have not even known of their existence. You can breakfast and dine well in them for less than half the price of similar meals in the large hotels. Ladies can go even alone to them with perfect propriety. They are to be found in all the principal thoroughfares of Paris, with the name of the founder, M. Duval, who was a butcher, over the door. Except in the principal one in the Rue Montesquieu, where the waiters are men, you are served by young women, all dressed alike in black, with a neat white cap, apron, and sleeves. In these

Bouillons too, Parisian life is to be seen in its best aspect. They are frequented chiefly by the respectable bourgeois with his wife and family, the steady student, and the man of business, who like to have what is good and wholesome, but who do not want to pay extravagantly for it.

We had a good deal of running about during the day making inquiries about circular tickets for Spain. There was no lack of routes to choose from, both from Paris and Irun, but eventually we decided to wait till we reached the latter station before taking our tickets for the Peninsula.

The next morning we left Paris for Bordeaux by the 8.45 express, and reached our destination in the evening, passing on the way many places notable in history, such as Orleans, Blois, Amboise, Poitiers, and Angoulême, but of which the *train rapide*, unmindful of the "mighty past," only allows the possibility of snatching a hasty glimpse. We shall not be hurried along quite so fast in Spain, and shall have plenty of time given us to ponder over the localities we pass through. Rain fell heavily at intervals during the journey, which rather spoilt the appearance of the country, although it conduced to our comfort in one way, by effectually laying the dust.

There is a fine theatre at Bordeaux, and the performances, next to those of Paris, are said to be the best in France. On walking out after dinner, we happened to pass the theatre, which was close to our hotel (*de France*). Halévy's opera, *Les Mousquetaires de la Reine*, was the piece announced for performance, and as it was just going to begin, we went in and heard two out of three acts.

In England little or nothing is known of Halévy, so I was glad of an opportunity of enlarging my slight acquaintance with him. *Les Mousquetaires de la Reine*, although hardly a classical, is nevertheless a melodious and pleasing work, and the instrumentation is skilful and appropriate, without being eccentric or overloaded. Both singers and orchestra on this occasion were efficient, and the performance was even, and showed no defects arising from a want of sufficient rehearsal. I wish the same could always be said of operatic performances in England. The company is,

I understand, a new one, so they were no doubt all on their good behaviour, like the new broom in the proverb.

Halévy, whose real name, H. Levy, proclaims his Jewish origin, although brought up on French soil, was not wanting in a cerain " Gründlichkeit," as the Germans call it, and his best works at least by no means deserve to be consigned to oblivion. I had heard a few years back the same author's *La Juive*, generally considered to be his masterpiece, finely done at the Grand Opera in Paris. But *Les Mousquetaires de la Reine* will perhaps be preferred by some. It is neither so pretentious nor so ponderous as *La Juive*.

But to proceed on our journey. We spent Sunday at Bayonne and Biarritz, both delightful places, and both interesting—the former especially, on account of its fine church, old castle, historical associations, and charming *grisettes* with their *mouchoirs coquettement arrangés* on their back hair. The towers of the cathedral have recently been reconstructed in admirable taste, and add greatly to the effect of the building, especially when seen from a little distance.

Next day we set out for Spain. On our way we passed the pleasant little sea-bathing place St. Jean de Luz, still boastful of having been the locality selected for the marriage of the Grand Monarch to the Infanta Maria Theresa in 1660. The picturesque Fuenterrabia, about which I hope to say something later on, is seen in the distance, just before entering Irun, the first Spanish town on the route. There our baggage was handed over to the mercy of the Spanish officials. But the examination did not prove such a formidable business as we expected. We had nothing to declare, and so were soon out of the clutches of the custom-house authorities.

Daylight happily remained with us sufficiently long after leaving the frontier to enable us to see the pretty harbour and village of Pasajes, and to catch glimpses, as the train jogged leisurely along, of the fine scenery of the country of the Spanish Basques, that singular race, the remnant of the earliest known inhabitants of the Peninsula. But unfortunately the grand, rocky, mountainous scenery of the Pancorbo district was hidden from our eyes by the darkness which set in some time before we reached that stern and inhospitable defile.

Our first halt was at Burgos, which we reached at 10.32 at night. I had sent a post-card for rooms from Bayonne, which the " boots " from the hotel produced on our arrival at the station ; and after a good jolting in an omnibus, we alighted in a short time at the *Fonda del Norte*—our first experience of a Spanish inn.

This *Fonda* is certainly a very second-rate establishment, but the beds were clean and comfortable, and the people civil and obliging. We were waited on by a charming little damsel, with a fresh rosy complexion, dark hair and eyes, and finely pencilled eyebrows, who did her best to please us. We had choco-late or coffee in the morning, breakfast at the *table-d'hôte* (*mesa redonda*) at eleven, and dinner at six—neither very first rate.

The streets of Burgos, although neither well paved nor well kept, are nevertheless not wanting in a certain marked character, severely and unmistakably Spanish, which naturally strikes the tourist fresh from Eng-land or the more frequented parts of the Con-

tinent. Their chief occupants during the
busy hours of the day are dark, sunburnt
peasants in broad-brimmed *sombreros*, short
jackets, breeches, with (or more often without)
gaiters, and with hempen sandals (*alpargatas*)
on their feet, leading or driving numerous
donkeys laden with fruit, vegetables, and
other marketable commodities. The *Plaza
Mayor*, or *Plaza de la Constitucion*, where the
market is held, has also a strong tinge of local
colour, especially in the morning, when it is
filled with buyers and sellers eagerly bar-
gaining. In the centre of the *Plaza* is a
bronze statue of Charles III., and it is surrounded by a colonnade, which affords hos-
pitable shelter in rainy weather. At the end
of the *Plaza* near the river is the Town-hall,
where repose the remains of that formidable
hero of early Castilian history, the Cid, and of
his wife, Ximena; and close by are pleasant
promenades, where are to be seen such rank,
beauty, and fashion as this ancient capital of
Old Castile can now assemble in these days of
its decline.

But the cathedral is of course the great
sight in Burgos, being one of the finest in

Spain—indeed in the world—and we spent many hours in examining its beauties. I leave the description of details to the professed ecclesiologist. Real lovers of architecture will find abundant food for contemplation in this superb church—so varied in style, and so rich in decoration both externally and internally. The most listless traveller can hardly fail to be struck with the exquisite beauty of the *cimborio,* or lantern, which rises above the crossing of the choir and transepts, and with the wonderful chapel of the Constable Don Pedro Fernandez de Velasco at the east end of the building. We explored most of the chapels, saw the coffer of the Cid, the gorgeous vestments of the altar and the clergy, the picture of a Magdalen attributed to Leonardo da Vinci, the little portable ivory altar which the Constable carried about with him in his campaigns, and other curiosities.

The coffer of the Cid is an antiquated trunk, one of two which that hero, in want of funds for the conquest of Valencia, is said to have filled with sand and pledged to two Jews of Burgos for a loan of 600 marks, making them believe it was full of valuables—a transaction which in the present day would most probably have brought " my Cid " under the notice of the *Guardia Civil.* He is said, however, to have honestly repaid both principal and interest.

The founder of the cathedral was Bishop Maurice, whose effigy is under a great lectern in the choir. He is stated to have been an Englishman by birth and to have been elected Bishop of Burgos in 1214. Juan de Colonia, a German by birth, is said to have designed the grand chapel of the Constable. " And it is not a little curious," as Street observes, " and perhaps not very gratifying to the *amour propre* of Spanish artists, that in this great church the two periods in which the most artistic vigour was shown, and the grandest architectural works undertaken, were marked, the first by the rule of a well travelled bishop—commonly said to be an Englishman—under an English princess, and who seems to have employed an Angevine architect; and the second by the rule of another travelled bishop, who, coming home from Germany, brought with him a German architect, into whose hands all the great works in the city seem at once to have been put." *

The beggars who haunt the doors of the churches, and indeed abound everywhere, present, it must be owned, a picturesque, but, at the same time, a decidedly *unsavoury* appearance. They look like second or third rate mummies, and their rusty old cloaks and tattered nether garments seem as if they might date from the time of the Cid. Burgos would appear to be the headquarters of rags and mendicity. The street boys, too, are a great trial. They follow you about in order to show you the way, and are by no means pleased if you do not accept their services. Nothing but a systematic and gentle course of *washing* and whipping would ever make these young wretches decent members of society.

Besides the cathedral we also went to the churches of St. Nicholas, where there is a superbly sculptured *retablo*, or altar-piece, and to Santa Gadea, or Agueda, a quaint little edifice, in which once upon a time the Cid forced Alphonso VI. to swear that he had

* 'Gothic Architecture in Spain,' chap. ii.

taken no part in the death of his brother Sancho; " and from that day forward," says the chronicle, " there was no love towards my Cid in the heart of the king." *   Here some hopeful young urchins thought proper to assail us with pebbles, pieces of plaster, and other missiles, as a punishment for our having refused to employ them in the capacity of *cicerones.*

We took a drive one afternoon to the *Cartuja de Miraflores,* about two miles out of town, which contains the beautiful tombs erected by Isabella the Catholic in memory of her parents Juan II. and Isabella of Portugal, and of her brother Don Alphonso, whose death in 1470 at the early age of sixteen, conferred the crown upon Isabella. The tombs are the work of Maestro Gil de Siloe, who commenced the work in 1489, and completed it in 1493. They are perfect marvels of elaborate workmanship, and deserve the closest inspection.

We were shown over the monastery by a Carthusian brother, one of three then in the place. The concern has not recently been in

* Southey's ' Chronicle of the Cid.'

a very flourishing condition ; but restorations are now being carried out, and the cells are soon to be filled again. Every monk has a cell, a bedroom, and a garden to himself, for silence and solitary confinement are the rule of the order, instead of sociability and usefulness to their fellow-creatures. " Mais il faut cultiver son jardin." If these gentlemen do not follow Candide's determination in this particular, they will find it, I fancy, rather difficult to keep away depression of spirits in their dreary abode.

Of the old castle but little now remains, except some dilapidated towers and ramparts, and a good specimen of a horse-shoe Moorish arch—a sample of many others we were afterwards to see. It must have been a strong fortress in the times of the early kings and counts of Castile. Many notable events have taken place within the walls of this once famous stronghold. Here Edward I. of England was married to Eleanor of Castile.

The Arco de Santa Maria is a most effective gateway ornamented with turrets and battlements, and adorned with statues of Nuño

Rasura, Lain Calvo, the Count Diego Porcello, Fernan Gonzales, the Cid, and Charles V., in honour of whom it is said to have been erected. From the opposite side of the bridge over the river Arlanzon leading up to this gateway, which is the principal entrance to the city, a fine view of the cathedral and its crocketed towers is obtained, with the gateway itself standing out majestically in the foreground.

The old mansions (*palacios*) too in Burgos are noteworthy specimens of the domestic architecture of the fifteenth and sixteenth centuries, especially the *Casa del Cordon*, which dates from the end of the fifteenth century. It has a fine *patio*, or inner court, with two tiers of galleries, and with trees and a fountain in the middle. All these old houses are decorated outside with the arms of their former owners. It is not, however, absolutely necessary to undertake a journey to Spain in order to study architecture of this description. Much the same sort of thing is still to be seen, although naturally on a more limited scale, in Galway, between which town and Spain a considerable commercial intercourse was at one time carried on. In Galway, too, as in Burgos, you will still find a considerable amount of superstition, with its usual accompaniments of dirt, backwardness, and beggary.

On Wednesday night we left damp, cold, dreary, but withal interesting Burgos for Madrid. Our slumbers by the way were softer and more balmy than slumbers during locomotion usually are. We were conscious of nothing till, on rubbing our eyes, between sleeping and waking next morning, we beheld rising on our left the immense convent-like mass of the Escorial, that " lugubre fantaisie du triste fils de Charles Quint," as M. Théophile Gautier appropriately calls it. We were soon in the dreary country surrounding Madrid, where there is little to relieve the monotony of the landscape except the view of the mountain range of the Sierra de Guadarrama. Our train reached the Spanish capital at 9.10 A.M. or thereabouts.

C

CHAPTER II.

MADRID.

MADRID is as different from Burgos as light from darkness. The latter dull, gloomy, and mediæval, the former bright, modern and Paris-like.

Our hotel was the *Fonda de los Embajadores*, in the *Calle de la Victoria*. Although recommended by the guide-books, we found it only moderately comfortable. The situation is good, although not actually on the *Puerta del Sol*, where most of the principal hotels are.

The chief thing to be seen in Madrid is, it need hardly be said, the Royal Picture Gallery, one of the finest, if not the very finest, in the world. No other, I fancy, has so many first-rate works by so many great masters. Velasquez is to be seen here, and here only, in all his power. Titian is here, too, in great force, as also Raffaelle, Veronese,

Murillo, Ribera, Juan Juanes, Goya, Rubens, Teniers, and many others. Rembrandt alone, of all the greatest artists, is not well represented. I could only find one picture by him, but it is a very fine specimen of his work; the subject is Queen Arthemisa about to swallow the ashes of her husband.

The streets of Madrid are clean and the houses well built. The so-called *Puerta del Sol* (literally *gateway of the sun*), in no sense now a gateway, but a public square, is the centre of life and animation of the city, indeed, of the whole of Spain itself; for here the various types which go to make up Spanish national life are to be met with, and may be studied, as it were, in epitome. Here all the principal streets meet, and from hence the numerous tramways, which traverse the city and suburbs in all directions, radiate as from a common centre. The square is consequently one continued scene of bustle and movement all day, and during a considerable portion of the night. The public walks are charming, especially the *Buen Retiro*, which is now the fashionable promenade, vice the *Prado* and the *Fuente Castellana*, superseded.

The carriages and horses of the Madrilenian high-life are as good as anything to be seen in Hyde Park or the Champs Elysées. The ladies of fashionable society dress as much as they can like French ladies, and discard for the most part the mantilla or veil. Their humbler sisters, however, still wisely retain the becoming national head-dress, and it is devoutly to be hoped that no caprice or change of fashion will ever induce a general abandonment of so charming a decoration. Spanish women enjoy a high reputation for grace and comeliness; let them beware, however, how they trifle with it. Dark sparkling eyes and rich jet black hair count doubtless for much, especially when found in conjunction with other equally potent natural attractions; but it may nevertheless, I think, be safely asserted that the ladies of Spain owe not a little of their justly acquired renown to the fascinating mantilla.

On the 16th of October I went to the Teatro de Apollo, one of the numerous theatres in Madrid. The *funcion* began at 8.30 P.M. I heard two acts of a " *Zarzuela* (Opéra Comique) en tres actos, letra de D. Mariano

Pina, Música del Maestro Rubio, titulada *El Corregidor de Almagro.*" The music, although not of a very high order, was bright and agreeable. Both singing and acting were good, and I could discover no weak points. I was especially struck with the way in which the chorus not only sang but *acted*, the latter quality being somewhat rare in a chorus. I was afterwards informed that the *Administrador* was very particular on this point. The orchestra, too, though small, was efficient and well balanced. The theatre is bright and well constructed. I was seated in a *butaca* (stall), for which I paid 14 reals (2*s.* 11*d.* in English money), and I heard and saw everything in the utmost comfort. There was no pit.

As now represented, the *Zarzuela* is nothing more nor less than an opéra comique in Spanish, and is a very popular form of entertainment in Spain. Ticknor gives an interesting account of the growth of the old *Zarzuela* in his ' History of Spanish Literature,' vol. ii. p. 293. The name, he tells us, was taken from one of the royal residences near Madrid, where they were represented with great splendour for the amusement of

Philip IV., by command of his brother Ferdinand.

Outside the theatres in Madrid a number of individuals will usually be seen congregated offering tickets for sale. It is advisable to ignore the existence of these touting gentlemen, and to go straight to the box-office and ask for the places you want, thus avoiding the possibility of extortion.

There is another peculiarity about Madrid theatres which deserves to be mentioned now that we are upon the subject. When the entertainment consists, say, of four short pieces, each followed perhaps by a ballet, constituting a performance, or *funcion*, as it is called, you are only called upon to pay for the particular *funcion* or *funciones* you desire to see, leaving the rest, not only unseen or unheard, but unpaid for; decidedly an economical arrangement for theatre-goers, such as does not, to my knowledge, exist in any other country.

On Sunday there was a bull-fight. We, as well as another lady and gentleman, whose acquaintance we had made at Burgos, went to it. The ladies went in merely to see the spectacle, and soon left, in which respect they acted wisely, for bull-fights are bloody and barbarous entertainments. They are, however, interesting from an antiquarian point of view, as they give some idea, imperfect though it may be, of what the old Roman gladiatorial shows must have been like. If it were worth the trouble an essay might easily be written on the resemblances between the ancient and modern show.

The new *Plaza de Toros* at Madrid is a magnificent building, and must be nearly as large in area as the Colosseum at Rome. It is constructed on much the same plan as the Roman amphitheatre. Those who go to Spain should see one bull-fight, but one will probably be found sufficient. It is, however, impossible to help admiring the skill of the performers. The *banderilleros* and *espadas* especially must be men of great activity, combined with complete presence of mind and bodily strength. How they escape being gored is to me a mystery. Sometimes, however, the bull is too much for them, and they suffer accordingly, occasionally with their lives, as was the case with the famous

Pepe Illo, whose unlucky end in the arena is the subject of one of the etchings of Goya in the series known as the Tauro-maquia.

Another unhappy victim was the great *espada*, Romero. He had, owing to numerous wounds received in the arena, for some years given up the honour of gratifying the amateurs of Madrid with exhibitions of his prowess. The queen of Charles IV., how-ever, who had always been an admirer of his skill, expressed a wish to see him perform once more. Romero mistrusted his luck; he did not wish, he said, to tempt Providence. His patroness ordered him to make the attempt. He obeyed, and was killed before the eyes of his royal admirer, having been empaled on the horns of the bull, who forth-with proceeded to gallop proudly round the ring with his victim, as if conscious of the importance of his triumph. Instances of similar tragic occurrences could doubtless be multiplied by those well up in the history of the subject. The professional bull-fighters have, for the most part, served their apprenticeship in the slaughter-house, so they are men familiar with bloody scenes from their youth. They have chosen their profession of their own free will. One does not, therefore, under ordinary circumstances, feel called upon to extend much compassion towards them.

The poor horses, on the other hand, are much to be pitied. This is the worst part of the business. The sufferings of the bulls must of course be intense, but one cannot help feeling the most for the wretched hacks, who are forced blindfold on to the very horns of the infuriated animals. At least ten horses were killed on this occasion ; one bull killed five " off his own horns." The more slaughter and bloodshed there is, the better the spectators seem to be pleased. Their excitement the whole time was intense, and their utter indifference to animal suffering extraordinary and brutish.

The king and two princes of Bavaria were present at this *corrida*, and remained, I believe, to the end of the performance, which is more than I did.

The bulls provided for the entertainment came from the celebrated herd of Don Antonio

Miura, near Seville. They were six in number, and names as usual were given to hem, which were as follows:—Cortijero, Rabituerlo, Cosario, Barbero, Beleto, and Cisquero. They were beautiful animals, with formidable horns, and swift of foot (*con buenas agujas y muchos pies*). It seemed a downright shame to torment and destroy them. Poor Cortijero, the first bull, was, in spite of appearances to the contrary, a quiet, well-disposed beast. He was considered a *bad* bull in consequence, and was accordingly condemned by the President "*a que le tostaran el morillo*," which sentence I prefer not to translate literally, but which means that instead of the darts used in ordinary cases those provided with *crackers* were inserted in this poor animal's neck, in order that by their explosion his rage might become excited. Sometimes, if this expedient fails to enrage the animal sufficiently, cries of "*Perros! perros!*" are heard on all sides, and dogs are introduced to worry him. I am happy to say I was not called upon to witness this piece of cruelty.

There seems no chance whatever of these

performances losing their popularity. One might as soon expect the Derby or the St. Leger to be given up as the Spanish bull-fight. Many Spaniards, however, disapprove of their "national sport" altogether, and never patronise it; but they are, of course, the exceptions.

The road to the *Toros* on these occasions is a sight in itself. Vehicles of every description are to be seen drawn by horses and mules in gay trappings, carrying people of all ranks and degrees, and of both sexes, the men being most numerous. The only thing approaching it is the road to Epsom on the Derby-day. Every kind of conveyance is called into requisition, from the one-horse cab to the eight-horse, or rather eight-mule, omnibus, and where they all come from is a mystery. Although gaily painted in bright colours, many of them are but crazy vehicles, and it is a matter of wonder that their crowded human freight ever arrives in safety, as the several Jehus drive furiously in order to make as many courses as possible before the show begins.

It rained during nearly the whole per-

formance, which naturally deprived the scene
of much of its usual brilliance.

In the newspapers of that evening, and of
the next day, accounts of the afternoon's
proceedings appeared as usual, written in the
customary slang of the arena, which I can
only compare to the language in which prize-
fights used not long since to be described in
' Bell's Life.'*   This *corrida* is said to have
been the best of the season, in spite of the
rain, which was so far satisfactory, as when
one has made up one's mind to be present at
any performance, it is as well that it should
be the best of its kind.

It is of course easy to moralise on the
subject of bull-fights. But it is fair to ask
whether more *actual suffering* is not inflicted
at a battue, a grouse or partridge drive, or
a pigeon match. The last is surely not a
very defensible form of sport, although ladies
have been known to grace it with their
presence; and what is to be said in favour of
prize-fighting, and other low and brutish
amusements which we have not long begun

* A specimen of this class of literature will be found at the
end of the volume.

to discountenance? Bull-fighting may be, and probably is, worse than any of these in its demoralising and hardening effects. But the question is after all only one of degree. Habit and custom, too, have much to do with regard to one's feelings in such matters.*

In the evening we were present at a *funcion* of a somewhat different nature, viz. a service of one of the six Spanish Protestant congregations at Madrid. It began at eight o'clock, and took place in a good-sized room in the *Calle Leyanitos.* The room was fairly well filled by a congregation consisting almost entirely of people of both sexes, belonging to the working classes. The form of service was similar to that adopted in Protestant churches in France, and lasted exactly an hour, including hymns, prayers, reading from the Bible, and a sermon. The clergyman had a clear and pleasant voice, and his delivery was very distinct and good. The people (except the babies, a few of which

* " An Englishman," says Byron, " who can be much pleased with seeing two men beat themselves to pieces, cannot bear to look at a horse galloping round an arena with his bowels trailing on the ground, and turns from the spectacle and the spectators with horror and disgust."—(Note to ' Childe Harold.')

were present) were very attentive and devout. The hymns were sung with considerable fervour; one of them was an adaptation of one of the most popular of those used by Messrs. Moody and Sankey. Some of the men present looked like brigands of the conventional type seen on the stage, as Spanish peasants not unfrequently do. One devout brigand offered me his hymn-book to read out of, an offer which I immediately accepted, so the brigand and I lifted up our voices together in the congregation.

The squalling kept up at intervals by the infants somewhat interfered with the harmony of the proceedings, notwithstanding all the maternal blandishments bestowed upon them, and the employment of other well-known methods of pacification usually effectual in such cases.

Not only in Madrid but in Seville, Cordova, and elsewhere there are Protestant congregations and schools. But whether this " little leaven " will be able to affect the prevailing religion, or whether scepticism or indifference will take root in Spain, as in France and other countries of Europe, in opposition to

any definite religious belief, are questions
which naturally present themselves to the
inquiring mind, but to which it is not so easy
to give an answer.*

* According to official returns laid before the Cortes in July
1876, the number of places of worship and schools of Spanish
Protestants were as follows : 53 places of worship ; 90 schools,
enrolled members 2500, and 8000 attendants at service on
Sundays at the various chapels ; 3000 children."—(' Statesman's
Year Book, 1881.') But what are they among so many !

CHAPTER III.

TOLEDO.

" The stranger cast around his curious eyes,
  New objects viewing still with new surprise,
  With greedy joy inquires of various things,
  And acts and monuments of ancient kings."
                    Dryden's *Virgil, Æneis*, viii.

But I find I have got a little out in my dates,
and have omitted to chronicle in its proper
place a most important event—I mean our
visit to Toledo. A journey to Spain without
a visit to Toledo would be something like a
performance of the tragedy of Hamlet with
the part of Hamlet left out, for in Toledo, all
or nearly all, the peculiarities of Spain are, so
to speak, concentrated.

We made an early start on Saturday morning, and arrived at our destination in time for
breakfast, which we found well and plenti-
fully provided at the *Fonda de Lino.*

The situation of Toledo, high upon a rock,

is most effective, and it is nearly surrounded by the Tagus. The view from the Alcántara bridge, which is crossed on the way from the railway station into the town, is wonderful. On each side is the rocky gorge of the river. Behind you is the ruined castle of San Servando, and in front the city rises with its quaint assemblage of buildings, and remains of old walls—the colossal Alcazar being the most elevated, and the most conspicuous object in the picture.

I was on the top of the omnibus, so saw everything to the best advantage. The 'bus was drawn by five mules, who appeared to know the way as well as their driver, and drew the vehicle up narrow crooked streets that seemed impassable to anything longer or wider than a wheelbarrow. It was extraordinary to see how these intelligent animals worked together, and refrained from treading on vegetables or earthenware exposed for sale in the streets we passed through. We were at length deposited safe and sound in the very courtyard of the inn.

We began our explorations as soon as breakfast was over, in company with a

D

German, who had brought a guide with him from Madrid, who forthwith hired another guide to show him the way. Guides are a necessary evil in Toledo, where there is so much to see, and where treasures of the past lie hid in unexpected places.

A prolonged stay would be necessary to enable the visitor to penetrate into every nook and corner of the imperial city; but a good general idea of its numerous treasures can be obtained in a comparatively short space of time, as the distances to be traversed are happily not great, and all, or at all events nearly all, the principal objects of interest lie closely grouped together.

We saw, I think, most of what was best worth seeing—the marvellous cathedral, the massive Alcazar, the beautiful Gothic church and cloisters of St. Juan de los Reyes, various Moorish and Gothic antiquities, and other wonders.

The cathedral unfortunately stands on low ground, and is much blocked up by buildings. There is, therefore, no good view of the exterior to be had. But the splendour of the interior, with its five naves, baffles description.

From whatever country the architect may have come, and it seems to be uncertain whether he was a Spaniard or a Frenchman, it is not unnatural that he should have been influenced to some extent by the prevailing architectural traditions of the place, and among the many and various subjects for study in this grand cathedral, certain peculiar Moresque details will not pass unnoticed by the observant.

The choir stalls, too, are most interesting, especially the lower range, the work of Maestro Rodrigo, about A.D. 1495, representing various incidents of the conquest of Granada. This wonderful specimen of grotesque carving doubtless gives a correct idea of the arms and accoutrements worn at the period, as the work was done only a few years after the conquest. It is worthy of notice that the high peaked saddles still used for the unfortunate steeds mounted by the picadors in the bull-fights are exactly the same as those represented on these stalls. The upper row, which dates from about the middle of the sixteenth century, is altogether different in style but interesting nevertheless. It is

*   D 2

the joint work of Berruguete and Felipe de Borgoña, who wrought in rivalry of each other, one taking one side and the other the other. Jasper pillars of a shining reddish brown colour divide the recesses of this wonderful construction.

The *rejas* (metal screens) and *retablos* are numerous, and for the most part admirable. The great *retablo* behind the high altar is filled with a multitude of statues and ornaments, all richly painted and gilded. This *retablo* is of great height, and is considered the best in Spain. It is certainly a superb example of this branch of ecclesiastical art.

There are chapels round the church as usual ; not the least interesting is the Mozarabic chapel, which stands to the right near the great western door. It is worth while, perhaps, telling over again the history of its foundation. The story is characteristic of mediæval times.

At the time of the Moorish invasion the inhabitants of Toledo were forced to surrender after a siege of two years. They endeavoured to capitulate on the most favourable terms, and one of the articles agreed upon was that

five (some say six) churches should be preserved for the use of the Christians who
desired to live with the conquerors. The
Christian faith was thus preserved in Toledo
during the four hundred years of Moorish
rule, and for this reason the faithful Toledans
were called Moz-arabs, i. e. "mixed with the
Arabs." In the reign of Alonzo VI., when
Toledo again came under Christian rule,
Richard, the Pope's legate, was anxious that
the Mozarabic rite should be abandoned in
favour of the Gregorian, and he was sustained
in his efforts by the king and the queen
Constanza, who preferred the rite of Rome.
The clergy and the people became furious in
consequence, and mutiny and revolution were
imminent. The king, alarmed at the turn
things had taken, and fearing that extreme
measures might be resorted to, calmed the
troubled spirits of the Toledans as best he
could, and proposed to them the following
singular compromise; which was quite in
keeping with the spirit of the times, and was
accepted with enthusiasm on both sides. The
partisans of the Mozarabic and Gregorian
rites were to choose champions, who were to

fight in order that God might make known which idiom and which ritual were the most acceptable to Him.

The name of the Mozarabic champion was Don Juan Ruiz de las Matanzas. A day was fixed. The Vega was chosen as the place for the encounter, and on the appointed signal being given the two antagonists spurred, lance in rest, to the charge. Victory remained for some time uncertain, but in the end Don Ruiz retired from the lists victorious. amidst shouts of delight from the Toledans, who forthwith betook themselves to the churches to kneel down, and offer up thanks and praises to Heaven. The king, the queen, and court, however, were very much annoyed at this triumph. Though rather late in the day, they gave out that they considered it an impious, rash, and cruel thing to have a theological question decided by a sanguinary combat, and proposed a new trial, which the Toledans, confident in the excellence of their ritual, accepted. The trial this time consisted, after a long fast and prayers in all the churches, in placing on a lighted bonfire copies of the Roman and Toledan rituals.

The one which should remain the longest in the flames without being burnt was to be considered the best and the most agreeable to God.

The programme was carried out exactly as arranged. A pile of dry and inflammable wood was set up on the Zocodover, the old Moorish square in the centre of the town, in the presence of an immense crowd of people. The two breviaries were thrown into the fire, each party offering up fervent prayers for the liturgy they preferred. The Roman ritual was thrown out of the fire either by the violence of the wind or the flames (authorities disagree on this point), and came out of the ordeal intact, but somewhat scorched. The Mozarabic ritual remained triumphantly in the midst of the flames in the place where it fell, without moving and without receiving any damage. The court was not quite pleased with the result, but there was no means of retracting, and thus the Mozarabic ritual was preserved in the city. It was kept up with ardour during many years, but at length the text ceased to be understood, and no one could be found who was able to understand or perform the office,

which had been the object of such eager
contests. When the great Ximenes became
Archbishop of Toledo, he determined to
preserve this interesting relic of faith, and
founded the chapel now in the cathedral. He
caused the ritual, which was in Gothic character, to be translated and printed in the
vulgar tongue, and instituted an order of
priests especially charged with the performance of the service.*

The chapel is adorned with most curious
and interesting frescoes, representing victories
over the Moors and the conquest of Oran.

Although I have not mentioned a quarter
of the treasures of art in the cathedral, I
must pass on to speak of other things.

The Alcazar is an imposing pile. It stands
on a lofty esplanade surrounded by ramparts,
from which an extensive view is obtained.
There is a fine court in the centre of the
building, which is now used as a military
school. It is intended to restore it to some-

* See also T. Gautier, ' Voyage en Espagne,' whose version of
this tradition of Toledo I have in the main followed. The
famous proverb, *Allá van leyes donde guiren reyes* (" There the
laws go where the kings show "), is considered to have arisen out
of this event.

what of its former grandeur, and elaborate restorations are now being carried out with great vigour.

The convent of San Juan de los Reyes was erected in 1476 by Ferdinand and Isabella in commemoration of their victory at Toro over the Portuguese in the then war of the succession. The walls of the church are adorned outside with a number of fetters and manacles of Christian captives rescued after the conquest of Granada—a species of decoration which produces, as may be supposed, a singular effect. Part of the convent is now used as a museum, over which we were shown. It contains, however, hardly anything but rubbish. These buildings are almost on the edge of a steep cliff overhanging the Tagus.

The cloisters, though much dilapidated, are perhaps the most attractive part of the convent. Here the florid Gothic style is to be seen in all its exuberance, and the effect produced by the architecture is still further heightened by the fresh green of the creeping plants that grow in the now desolate garden in the centre, and climb caressingly round the delicate half-ruined stonework.

Near this convent are the remains of the palace of the Gothic kings, from a window in which Roderick, the last of the Goths, is said to have seen Florinda, the fair daughter of Count Julian, bathing in the river below, an indiscretion which led to the invasion of the Moors and the destruction of Roderick's kingdom. Roderick fell in love with the imprudent bather and effected her ruin. The Count, her father, was naturally furious, and betrayed his country to the Moors by way of vengeance. All which furnished cause of grievous lamentation to the said Don Roderick. He afterwards repented, not in sackcloth and ashes, but in a tomb with a viper, which gnawed him to death. Such at least was his fate if we are to believe popular tradition and romance. Sober history, however, to which doubtless some weight must be allowed in such matters, would persuade us that King Roderick perished with the flower of his nobility in the fatal battle of Xerez in 711, and that the causes which have been popularly and romantically assigned for his overthrow, have little if any foundation in fact.

The river is here crossed by the fine old bridge of San Martin, flanked at each end by battlemented towers. It consists of five arches, of which the central one is the largest, being no less than 140 (Spanish) feet wide, by 95 feet high from the level of the waters.

It has been more than once rebuilt. During the civil commotions that agitated the reign of Pedro the Cruel it was broken down by the insurgents in order to place the river between themselves and their enemies, and it was not till about the year 1390 that Archbishop Pedro Tenorio, who did much for the improvement of the city, sent for a celebrated architect and entrusted him with the restoration of the structure.

To this noble bridge, as to so many other monuments of Toledo, a curious old popular tradition is attached.

When the work of restoration above referred to was approaching its completion, the architect to his dismay discovered that he had made a mistake in his calculations, and that as soon as the scaffolding was removed the whole structure would inevitably fall to pieces. He was seized with melancholy in consequence, for his reputation would naturally suffer, and ruin would stare him in the face. He was, however, so fortunate as to possess a wife as devoted as she was ingenious, who hit on a novel plan for saving her husband's reputation. She sallied forth at night with a flaming torch in her hand and set fire to the woodwork. Scaffolding and stonework all fell together, and the unsophisticated Toledans attributed the calamity to an accidental fire. The work was begun again forthwith on sounder principles, and when it was finished this clever lady went to the archbishop and confessed everything. But he, instead of upbraiding her, only commended the means she had adopted to save her husband's character as an architect from dishonour.

The two old Jewish synagogues, now called El Transito and Santa Maria la Blanca, are most curious and interesting. They are situated in the quarter of the town formerly inhabited by the Jews before their final expulsion, after much previous persecution, in 1492. Both buildings are in the Saracenic style of architecture, and doubtless Moorish workmen were engaged in their erection. El

Transito was erected by Samuel Levi, a rich
Jew, who was treasurer to Peter the Cruel,
and was completed in 1366 ; but at the expulsion of the Jews it was given by Ferdinand
and Isabella to the military order of Calatrava.

A singular tale is told of these Toledan
Jews which may appropriately be inserted
here. It is thus given by Southey :—" When
Toledo was recovered from the Moors by
Alonzo VI., the Jews of that city waited upon
the conqueror and assured him that they were
part of the ten tribes whom Nebuchadnezzar
had transported into Spain ; not the descendants of the Jerusalem Jews who had crucified
Christ. Their ancestors, they said, were
entirely innocent of the crucifixion ; for when
Caiaphas the high priest had written to the
Toledan synagogues to ask their advice
respecting the person who called himself the
Messiah, and whether he should be slain, the
Toledan Jews returned for answer that in
their judgment the prophecies seemed to be
fulfilled in this person, and therefore he ought
not by any means to be put to death. This
reply they produced in the original Hebrew
and in Arabic, as it had been translated by

command of King Galifre. Alonzo gave ear
to the story, had the letter rendered into Latin
and Castilian, and deposited it among the
archives of Toledo." (Note to ' Roderick.')

We also saw the beautiful hospital of Santa
Cruz, which was originally a hospital for
foundlings. It was endowed by the great
Cardinal Mendoza, who died in 1495, and its
erection was superintended by Isabella, who
condescended to act as the cardinal's trustee.
Such an institution appears by all accounts to
have been much needed in those days in
Spain, and the cardinal thought, perhaps, that
by endowing a foundling hospital he might
succeed in atoning for certain youthful indis-
cretions laid to his charge by historians.
There are beautiful *patios* and a remarkable
staircase in the building ; the latter has an
artesonado* roof, of exquisite workmanship.
The *façade*, through a door in the centre of
which the building is entered, is an admirable
specimen of the so-called plateresque or renaissance style of architecture.

---

* *Artesonado*, in the form of a trough, from *artesa*, a knead-
ing-trough, an expression applied to carved ceilings, the ornamentation of which takes the form of inverted troughs.

The gates and walls of Toledo are well worthy of inspection. Of the gates the two most interesting are the famous *Puerta del Sol* and the old *Puerta de Visagra*, both in pure Saracenic style. The first dates from about the end of the twelfth or beginning of the thirteenth century, and "is indeed," as Street says, "not only picturesque, but in all respects a dignified and noble work of art." The view from it, too, over the *Vega* beneath is very grand. The old *Puerta de Visagra* is still more ancient, and may be considered to date from the end of the ninth century. Through it on Sunday, the 25th of May, 1085, Alonzo VI. made his triumphal entry into Toledo on the recovery of the city from the Moors.

But everything in Toledo is interesting, and every house seems centuries old, and looks as if it had or ought to have a history all to itself. The doors of many of the houses and convents cannot fail to attract notice as you pass through the narrow, winding, oriental-looking streets, for they are thickly studded with great nails, and are provided with knockers in most grotesque designs. It is impossible even for the most unimpressionable tourist to help being struck by the remarkable character of everything in the place. But for any one of an artistic, romantic, or antiquarian turn of mind Toledo is a perfect mine of wealth. "Few cities that I have ever seen," says Street, with justifiable enthusiasm, "can compete in artistic interest with it, and none, perhaps, come up to it in the singular magnificence of its situation, and the endless novelty and picturesqueness of its every corner. It epitomises the whole strange history of Spain in a manner so vivid, that he who visits its old nooks and corners carefully and thoughtfully, can work out almost unassisted the strange variety which that history affords. For here Romans, Visigoths, Saracens, and Christians have in turn held sway, and here all have left their mark; here, moreover, the Christians since the thirteenth century have shown two opposite examples, one of toleration of Jews and Moors, which it would be hard to find a parallel for among ourselves, and the other of intolerance, such as has no parallel out of Spain."

We were reluctantly compelled to return to Madrid by the afternoon train.

A direct line of railway now runs between Madrid and Toledo. The distance between the two places is only 44½ English miles, but the time consumed in traversing it is nearly three hours. Formerly it was necessary to go round by Castillejo. The country passed through is very uninteresting, and had, at least when we saw it, a dry and parched appearance. Indeed, nothing is met with to break the monotony of the landscape, or what does duty for such, until Toledo is reached. There, however, you are richly rewarded.

CHAPTER IV.

CORDOVA.

WE did not remain much longer in Madrid. There is really not a very great deal to see there beyond the famous picture gallery and the *Armeria.* The latter was closed the day we presented ourselves for admission, so we missed seeing it, which we much regretted, as we were very anxious to inspect the curious armour and other relics there exposed to view. We did our duty, however, towards Madrid in other respects, and drove and walked much up and down through most parts of it. We sat some time ruminating in the antiquated *Plaza Mayor*, where formerly many Jews, heretics, and atheists were tortured and burnt in the *autos da fé*, with a view to the promotion of Christian knowledge and the discountenance of wickedness and vice, which desirable objects, however, were little, if at all, advanced by such proceedings. Here bull-feasts used to take place, at the time when there were few, if any, professional bull-fighters, and young noblemen and gentlemen charged, or rather were charged by, ferocious bulls, with a view of making themselves acceptable to their mistresses, who looked on during the exciting spectacle from the balconies above. Here Charles I., when Prince of Wales, was treated to a bull-feast when he was paying his respects to his affianced bride, the Infanta Maria.

In connection with the bull-feasts that used in former days to be given in this *Plaza*, I cannot forbear inserting here an affecting story which I alighted upon one day by chance in a singular book called the 'History of the Female Sex.' It is as follows :—

" The greatest and most dangerous proof of love for a man, was to fight a wild bull in honour of his mistress.* Cavaliers begged permission of their ladies to engage in these fights. During the conflict, the ladies waved their handkerchiefs in token of approbation ; and when the cavaliers had vanquished their antagonists, they made a low obeisance to the

* D'Aunoy's ' Letters,' pp. 186–189.

objects of their passion, and kissed their
swords with which they had killed, or
mortally wounded, the bulls. These fights
in honour of their ladies cost many a Spanish
gentleman his life. A few years before
Madame D'Aunoy visited Spain, a young
cavalier heard that some of the most ferocious
bulls of the mountains were taken, and were
kept for an approaching fight. This intelli-
gence inspired the intrepid youth with the
wish to acquire honour for himself and his
intended bride, in an engagement with one of
these formidable animals. He acquainted his
mistress with his design; and she, by the
most affecting entreaties, endeavoured to dis-
suade him from his purpose. All her prayers
and all her remonstrances were in vain.
Athirst for glory, the lover entered the lists
with others of his own rank and age, and
engaged one of the first and largest bulls that
was let loose. The fight had scarcely begun,
when a stranger, in the dress of a peasant,
advanced, and with a dart gave the bull a
painful wound. Quitting his first antagonist,
the furious animal rushed upon his new
adversary, whom he immediately extended

with a mortal blow upon the ground. In falling, the long and beautiful hair of the youth was exposed by the loss of his cap; and it appeared that the uninvited enemy of the wounded bull was a young female, and the bride of the cavalier who had determined to fight in honour of her. The bridegroom, rendered desperate by this spectacle, defended his mistress bathed in blood, with astonishing heroism. He likewise received several mortal wounds.

" The unfortunate lovers were placed in the same chamber, where, at their request, the nuptial ceremony was performed, and in a few hours they both expired."

The *Plaza* is now a public square, and is resorted to chiefly by the working classes, and by purveyors of water, sweetmeats, and lucifer matches. In the centre stands a fine equestrian statue of Philip III., by Juan de Bologua. In the *Plaza Oriente*, near the Royal Palace, is the still finer and more spirited equestrian statue of Philip IV., executed after the famous portrait by Velazquez, in the Royal Picture Gallery. The great Galileo is said to have suggested the means whereby the horse is balanced on his hind legs. You naturally expect a statue modelled after Velazquez, and poised by the aid of Galileo, to be something worth looking at, and you are not disappointed, for the monument is one of the finest of its kind in existence.

On Monday, the 18th of October, we left Madrid for Cordova by the evening express, and arrived at our destination early next morning. We found the hotel, the *Fonda Suiza,* very good, clean, and comfortable. There is a pleasant *patio* in the middle, with a beautiful marble floor, and adorned with trees and fountains, as is customary in Andalusia. The staircase of the hotel is also marble, and has a different pattern of mosaic on each landing, admirably worked. In fact, the whole building was more like the residence of a grandee than a house of entertainment for the reception of travellers.

The chief annoyance in connection with Cordova is the excessive difficulty in finding one's way about. The streets are so numerous and so narrow, that it is next to impossible to know where you are. We were beset with

guides in consequence, who know the diffi-
culties of the place, and take advantage of
them. We found ourselves at last forced to
accept the services of a youth, who persisted
in pursuing us. With his help we found out
all we wanted to see. These youths, although
a decided nuisance, are not, it must be owned,
altogether useless; for besides showing you
where to go, they serve as a *corpus vile*, on
which to experimentalise with a view to the
purification of indifferent Castilian.

Our steps were naturally directed in the
first instance to the world-famed mosque.
On our way we passed a fine old Roman
gate, the name of which I do not at this
moment recall. We first walked through the
beautiful court of oranges, where a cistern
for ablution, erected in 945 by Abderrahman,
still stands, and where shady palms and
orange trees flourish under the balmy sky.
From the court we entered the mosque itself.
The effect produced by the numerous columns
is at first quite bewildering, but at the same
time most striking, although one misses the
extent of view which is such a beautiful
feature of fine Gothic interiors. There are

said to have been at one time 1200 of these pillars, and there are still nearly 1000. They are of the most beautiful marbles, of different kinds and colours, and they divide the building into nineteen naves one way, and twenty-nine the other. The ornamentation of the *Mihrab*, or sanctuary of the mosque, where the Koran was kept, is something marvellous. But the character of the whole building has been much spoiled by the construction of a choir in the centre in the sixteenth century. This choir may be all very well in its way, and would perhaps produce effect with suit-able surroundings, but here it is utterly out of place. Unfortunately Charles V., unaware at the time of what he was doing, allowed the works to be carried out. But when he visited Cordova in 1526, he discovered, though too late, the piece of vandalism which had been committed. " I was not aware of this," he cried, " for had I known you intended to touch the ancient portion, I would not have permitted it. You have built here what can be built anywhere else, but you have de-stroyed what was unique in the world." The original Moorish roof has been taken away.

It was higher than the present one, and is said to have been profusely decorated with vivid colours. The floor is also higher than it used to be; consequently the building is much too low for its size. Whitewash, moreover, has effaced a good deal, so that the original glory of the mosque, as it must have appeared when thousands of gold and silver lamps were burning, and the polished marble columns and gorgeous ornamentation glistened in the light, can now only be imagined. Enough, however, still remains to enable the visitor to form some idea of its pristine splendour.

Near the mosque the Guadalquivir (Betis) rolls " his glittering stream," that is to say, whenever he has any stream to roll, for not unfrequently his bed is totally dry through drought, or from the waters having been abstracted for the purposes of irrigation. The river is here crossed by an interesting old bridge, built originally by the Romans, but reconstructed by the Arabs. The opposite end of the bridge is guarded by the picturesque old battlemented fortress known as the Calahorra Tower, and in the river close by are the quaint remains of some old Moorish mills, which give additional character to the remarkable scene.

Cordova is now but a ghost of its former self. If we are to credit the statements of Moorish chroniclers, at the time of its greatest prosperity, at the end of the ninth and the beginning of the tenth century, it possessed 1600 mosques, 900 baths, 80,455 shops, 262,300 houses, and a population not far short of 1,000,000. It was then the successful rival of Bagdad and Damascus, and the home of lite-rature, science, and art,* whereas now but few traces of its former magnificence remain. In the day time the narrow streets seem deserted, except by donkeys laden with jars of water and other burdens, and their two-legged

---

* The accounts which have come down to us of the splendour of Cordova when it was the metropolis of Arabian Spain are quite bewildering, and we should feel inclined to consider them open to question if their substantial accuracy were not confirmed by comparing them with accounts of palaces and other buildings still in existence, which are found on examination to be correct and trustworthy. For a full description of the ancient city and its suburbs, at the height of its greatness, including the gorgeous palace of Azzahra (the Flower), built by the Caliph Annasir, and named after his favourite mistress, see the appendix to Washington Irving's 'Tales of the Alhambra,' by the Rev. Hart-well Horne.

attendants. But Cordova is not quite such a city of the dead as might at first sight be imagined. Go out after sunset and you will behold a different scene. There is then plenty of animation and movement. The shops are lighted up and the people are all astir. Lovers meet their mistresses, or stand opposite the iron bars of their windows and talk to the fair one within. I did not venture out alone, not that there was any fear of being robbed or murdered, but only the certainty that I should lose my way in the labyrinth of lanes and alleys which go to make up the city. But a French gentleman, whose acquaintance we had made, knew some of the Spanish residents, and these gentlemen were so kind as to take us out in the evening for an airing.

After having been regaled at a café, we were taken over the casino, or club. Without doubt things are not always what they seem, and a stranger would little dream of the existence of such an admirable club in so oriental-looking a city as Cordova. Facts, however, must not be moulded to suit preconceived theories, and certainly this casino will bear comparison, as regards convenience

and comfort, with any of the best establishments in Pall Mall, allowance being of course
made for the difference in the internal
arrangements consequent on the dissimilarity
in the climates of the two countries. The
premises cover a large space of ground, and,
in addition to several good rooms, the club
possesses a magnificent ball or concert room,
and some pleasant *patios*. When balls are
given these *patios* are lighted up, and the
dancers can walk about and refresh themselves in them between the dances. The
genial climate of Andalusia allows, I should
rather say encourages, nocturnal flirtations in
the open air, even in the month of February.

We are now in the land of *patios*, oranges,
and engaging damsels with flowers neatly set
in their long dark hair. The weather is
superb, the sky blue and clear all day, and
the nights moonlit. The effect of the moon-
light in the narrow whitewashed streets is
very charming. The air is soft, and there is
no wind. The mosquitoes are the only draw-
back to our enjoyment. We had a whole
hive of them in our room, and, as our beds
had no mosquito curtains, we were most

unmercifully bitten ; we looked when we got
up next morning as if we were going to have
the smallpox.

I ̦have already made use of the word
patio more than once ; and, as it is a word of
frequent occurrence whenever the subject of
life in Andalusia is under consideration, it
may not, perhaps, be out of place to attempt
a definition of it for the benefit of those who
have not yet had an opportunity of visiting
that much-favoured province. A *patio* may,
I think, be defined as an inner court, or four-
sided saloon, placed in the centre of a building,
but having no other permanent roof than the
azure vault of the heavens. It is generally
separated from the street by a vestibule paved
with black and white marble, and terminated
within by a wrought-iron gateway artistically
designed. All around the *patio*, which is also
paved with marble like the vestibule, there
runs a gallery resting on semicircular or
Moorish arches supported by slender columns.
This gallery is the upper story of the house.
The ground-floor is used for the dwelling-
place in summer, and the *patio* then serves as
the drawing-room where the family meets,

and friends are received. During the heat
of the day a canvas covering is stretched
from the top of the gallery across the whole
court, as a shelter from the burning rays of
the sun, and the *patio* is kept fresh and cool
by means of skilfully managed currents of
air, and by a fountain which plays and
bubbles in the middle. All around orange
trees, aloes, and creeping plants, and flowers
are tastefully arranged. The household furniture is brought down from the upper rooms
for the summer season, and much taste is
shown in the general decoration. In the
evening the canvas is withdrawn, and the
lamps hanging round the walls are lighted,
whereby effects are produced such as one
would hardly expect to meet with on this
side of fairyland. Indeed, life in an Andalusian dwelling would appear to be the perfection
of existence. When we were in the province
the inhabitants were gradually moving their
furniture and effects back to the upper rooms
for the winter.

CHAPTER V.

SEVILLE.

" Nach Sevilla, nach Sevilla,
  Wo die letzten Häuse stehen,
  Sich die Nachbarn freundlich grüssen,
  Mädchen aus dem Fenster sehen,
  Ihre Blumen zu begiessen,
  Ach, da sehnt mein Herz sich hin ! "
                                    BRENTANO.

THE express to Cordova and Seville goes at
night, and consequently we missed seeing the
classic ground of La Mancha through which
the line passes. However, it is to be presumed
that this part of Spain is not unlike many
other parts, and one can imagine the illustrious Hidalgo tilting at sheep and windmills
in almost any part of the country we have
seen, except the Basque provinces, which are
far too mountainous for such exalted feats of
chivalry. I could see too, "in my mind's
eye, Horatio !" the faithful Sancho tossed in a
blanket in several courtyards, and we passed

by not a few *ventas,* any of which his redoubt-
able master might have fancied to be a
"castle fenced with four towers, and lofty
pinnacles glittering with silver, together with
a deep moat, drawbridge, and all those other
appurtenances peculiar to such kind of
places."

Real castles, or rather the ruins of them,
are, however, to be seen in considerable
abundance in all parts of the country. These
genuine "châteaux en Espagne" offer a fine
field for the explorer, which has not as yet
been properly examined and illustrated.*
On the way to Seville next day we passed
a very good specimen, finely situated on the
slopes of a lofty hill above the town of
Almodovar. This castle is associated with
the name of the infamous Pedro the Cruel, by
whom it was fortified and used as a place of confinement. It is now little more than a ruin,
but it is none the less on that account a highly
picturesque and striking object. The country
here abounds in oranges, olives, aloes, and
cactuses, and many of the aloes are in flower.

* For an account of some of the ruined castles in the district
round Toledo see N. A. Wells' ' Picturesque Antiquities of Spain.'

We reached Seville in the afternoon, and found very comfortable quarters at the Hôtel de Madrid. Our bedroom was on the ground-floor, very clean and nicely furnished, but a trifle noisy, owing to its proximity to the street. Our beds had mosquito curtains, so we were not bitten so fearfully as at Cordova. Here again we found a splendid *patio* full of bananas and palm trees, which in these favoured regions grow luxuriantly in the open air, but in England require artificial heat to make them grow at all.

Seville, in addition to its many other attractions, is the place above all others where Murillo can best be studied. His very finest works are to be seen in the picture gallery, the Convent of *La Caridad*, and the cathedral. Zurbaran's greatest picture, the Apotheosis of St. Thomas Aquinas, is also in the picture-gallery. Unfortunately the interior of the magnificent cathedral is so dark that the pictures in it are almost invisible. Murillo's famous picture of St. Anthony of Padua is in the baptistry. For this great work the artist is said to have received the sum of 10,000r. (about 100l.), which sounds but a

F

modest amount to our ears. The same painter's Holy Family and the St. John and the Lamb in the National Gallery cost, the former about 4000 guineas, and the latter 2000 guineas. So it has been also with the violins of Stradivarius. They were sold originally for about 4*l.* apiece, whereas now 400*l.* would not be thought an excessive price for a perfect specimen of the master's work.

Various sacred buildings have occupied the site of the present cathedral. First there appears to have been a temple to Venus Salambo, at one time the fashionable deity of the Sevillians, then a Christian church (the *Basilica de San Vicente*), which in its turn gave place to a splendid mosque on the plan of the one at Cordova. After this came a second and last mosque, built by the Emir Yusuf in 1184, which lasted till 1401. The Chapter then met and heroically determined on erecting a church "so large and beautiful, that coming ages might proclaim them mad to have undertaken it." The old building had been converted into a cathedral by St. Ferdinand. It had been frequently repaired and altered; and as it now threatened to cease to exist altogether, it was pulled down, and the cathedral we now see begun. Of the old mosque nothing now remains but the lower part of the beautiful Giralda Tower, the Court of the Oranges, and portions of the outer walls. The upper part of the tower was added by Hernan Ruiz in 1568, who inscribed thereon in large letters the words " *Turris fortissima nomen Domini,*" from the Book of Proverbs. The tower is crowned by a gigantic female figure in bronze representing *Faith*, which instead of remaining, as it is emblematically supposed to do, immovable, turns with the breath of every wind of heaven.

The *Puerta del Perdon*, a beautiful horseshoe arch, through which you enter the Court of the Oranges from the north, forms part of the outer walls above referred to. The old bronze Moorish doors still remain in a good state of preservation. In the court is still to be seen one of the fountains where the devout Mussulmans were accustomed to perform their ablutions before they entered the Grand Mosque. Here is also the stone pulpit from which St. Vicente Ferrer preached. The

message delivered by this ecclesiastic does not
appear to have been by any means one of
" peace " and " love," but on the contrary one
much in favour of flames and tortures for
Jews and all so-called heretics.   He is stated,
moreover, to have performed innumerable
miracles, and these doubtless, added to his
zeal for the " true faith," procured him the
honour of canonisation.

Near the cathedral are the *Lonja* or
Exchange, containing the valuable documents
by Columbus, Cortez, and Pizarro, relating to
America, and the famous Alcazar, in the style
of, and but little inferior to, the Alhambra,
although its position can in no way compare
with the commanding site of the latter palace.
It was restored and in great part rebuilt by
Pedro the Cruel ; and subsequent monarchs,
notably Charles V., have each had a share in
the work of restoration.   But in spite of all
the transformations it has from time to time
undergone, enough is still left to excite in the
beholder feelings of astonishment, as he
wanders through its courts and halls, now
only filled with reminiscences of famous and
infamous deeds of bygone days.   Here Pedro

perpetrated many of his atrocities. The catalogue of the crimes laid to the charge of this prince is a long one. His worst act was, perhaps, his treachery to the *Rey Bermejo* (the red king) of Granada, who sought refuge at his court. The red king, unfortunately for himself, brought with him his wonderful collection of jewels, which so excited the cupidity of Pedro that he caused his guest to be murdered and got possession of his gems. Among them was the large ruby which Pedro gave to the Black Prince after the battle of Navarrete, and which now adorns the royal crown of England. This is " the fair ruby, great like a racket-ball," which Elizabeth showed to Sir James Melville, the ambassador of Mary of Scotland, who was very anxious that it should be sent " as a token unto the queen," his mistress.

Behind the Alcazar are the beautiful gardens in the cinquecento style laid out by Charles V. Here are terraces, fountains, hedges of myrtle, orange trees, and flowers of various kinds; and brilliant sunshine is not wanting to add to the surrounding charms. You feel while in this delightful place as if

life could have no cares, and that mere existence is a pleasure in itself; and you will be,
perhaps, somewhat disposed to wonder why
the emperor could not have been satisfied to
dream away the latter days of his life in so
fairy-like a retreat, instead of morosely seeking
the monastic seclusion of the convent at Yuste.
In a corner near the entrance we were shown
the bath of the fascinating Maria Padilla, the
favourite mistress of Pedro. The bath is in
an arched crypt, with a hole in the top,
through which Pedro is said to have gazed on
the comely form of the fair bather.

Not far off are the fashionable promenades
on the banks of the Guadalquivir, where the
Sevillian beauties

    " *Spectatum veniunt, veniunt spectentur ut ipsœ,*"

as beauties have done, and will continue to do,
in all ages, and in every country under the
sun.

The *Torre del Oro,* or Tower of Gold, so
called either from its former colouring or
because gold was said to have been deposited
in it by the Arabs, is also nigh at hand. It
was used by turns as a prison and a treasure

house by Pedro, but it now serves the commonplace purpose of a navigation office. On the
opposite side of the river is the suburb of
Triana, the abode of smugglers, gipsies, bull-
fighters, and ragged boys such as Murillo
used to paint.

Adjoining the promenades are the fine
modern palace and gardens of San Telmo,
belonging to the Duke of Montpensier.

On the other side of the city is the ancient
and extensive, but now deserted, *Alameda* (or
Promenade) *de Hercules.* At the entrance to
it are two lofty granite columns, very old,
and much worn away by time. On one of
them is placed the statue of Hercules, who
was the reputed founder of Seville, and who
shared with the aforesaid Venus the devotions
of the inhabitants. The other is surmounted
by a statue of Julius Cæsar. This promenade
is only, so to speak, galvanized into life once
a year at Midsummer, viz. on the eve of the
festival of St. John (*la velada·de San Juan*),
when flirtation and festivity are the order,
not of the day, for it would certainly be too
hot, but of the night as long as it lasts.

Seville, like Cadiz, was formerly a Phœnician colony; and although a discussion on the obscure subject of Syrian mythology would be out of place here, it is worth observing, perhaps, that the worship of the Venus above referred to was imported from Syria, and that the goddess in question was none other than the Syrian Astarte or Ashtoreth, whom the " wise " king Solomon foolishly " went after " in his old age, as we read in 1 Kings xi. 5.* We shall not, perhaps, be much astonished at his want of religious stability if we take into consideration the circumstances that turned his head, as recorded in verse 3 of the same chapter. Those enthusiastic young ladies, the Saints Justa and Rufina, on the other hand, would have none of this profane worship, and flatly refused to bow down to the idols of the goddess when carried in procession through the Triana. Whereupon a rude mob fell upon them and slew them, smashing at the same time their stock-in-trade of earthenware, by the sale of which they gained their livelihood. Considering their zeal in the cause of Christianity while they were alive, it

---

* It is scarcely necessary to refer to Milton's poetical account of this worship in Book I. of the ' Paradise Lost.'

is somewhat astonishing to find them after death the defenders of the Giralda Tower, which is not a Christian, but an Arab, and consequently a Mahommedan structure.

We did not go over the Government tobacco manufactory, which is near the Palace of San Telmo, although I believe it is well worth seeing. Between five and six thousand women are employed there daily.

The streets of Seville are a sight in themselves. They are, perhaps, wider than those at Cordova, and the houses are higher, but otherwise the same characteristics prevail. We spent a good deal of our time prowling about them, which we were allowed to do, I am glad to say, without molestation from guides or *gamins*.

I wonder more people do not come to spend the winter in Seville. It is without doubt a charming place, and rich in art treasures and historical associations. It is as clean as a Dutch town—too clean, indeed, for the enthusiastic archæologist, who would prefer rather less whitewash. The hotels and cafés are excellent, and the climate well-nigh perfection. It rains, however, sometimes, and when it does come down there is no mistake about it. We had one wet day while we were there, and it rained in torrents. But it is soon over, and then sun and clear sky begin to bear rule again.

The race of barbers is not yet extinct in Seville, but the shop of the famous Figaro, immortalised by Beaumarchais, Mozart, and Rossini, no longer exists. It used, *it is said*, to stand in the *Plaza San Tomas*, not far from the cathedral. If a barber's shop were again started on the old premises, it ought, I should think, to do a good business.

CHAPTER VI.

Our stay in "proud Seville" over, we left it for Granada. A railway now connects the two places by way of Utrera, La Roda, and Bobadilla, at each of which stations we had to change carriages,* much to our annoyance. But our luggage was booked and registered

---

* As will be seen from the following extract from a recent number of the Spanish Official Railway Guide, first-class passengers no longer change carriages between Seville and Granada, and *vice-versâ* :—

Servicio de Cádiz y Sevilla á Málaga y Granada y *vice-versâ*.

Estaciones.		Horas.	Estaciones.		Horas.
Cádiz	Sal	m 6·00	Granada	Sal	m 5·30
Sevilla	Sal	7·30	Málaga	Sal	7·30
Utrera	{Lleg	8·29	Bobadilla ..	{Lleg	9·47
	{Sal	10·00		{Sal	10·07
La Roda	{Lleg	t 2·20	La Roda	{Lleg	10·45
	{Sal	3·06		{Sal	11·05
Bobadilla ..	{Lleg	3·13	Utrera	{Lleg	t 3·00
	{Sal	4·03		{Sal	3·14
Málaga	Lleg	6·06	Sevilla	.. ..	4·05
Granada	Lleg	n 8·20	Cádiz	.. ..	n 7·36

Los viajeros de 1ª clase entre Sevilla y Granada y *vice-versâ* no cambiarán de coche.

the whole way through, so we had no occasion
to trouble ourselves about it. The journey
took up the entire day, and the train crawled
lazily along, thus giving us ample opportunity
to see the country and places through which
we passed. It is decidedly an advantage, I
think, to dawdle along through a country like
this, bristling, as it literally does, with historical associations and romantic interest. You
are thus given time to collect your ideas and
duly to ponder over the objects you pass,
instead of being whisked by them as if they
were not worthy of attention.

At Marchena are still to be seen considerable
remains of strong Moorish fortifications. The
whole town has a decidedly stern and oriental
appearance. At the old stronghold of Antequera there are still vestiges of the Roman
and the Moor.

Loja is most romantically situated on the
banks of the Genil, at the opening of the
mountains encircling the Plain of Granada;
and although now decayed, it is full of interest,
owing chiefly to the notable siege it sustained
in the war of Granada, when Lord Rivers
and his English archers rendered such impor-

tant aid to Ferdinand and his army in this last struggle against the hated Moor. The great captain, Gonsalvo de Cordova, retired to this place in consequence of the neglect shown to him by Ferdinand, and spent there the remainder of his days in a seclusion neither unpleasant to himself nor unprofitable to others.

Near Antequera the train passes a huge rock, *La Peña de los Enamorados*, or Lovers' rock, which, as may be suspected from its name, has a romantic story attached to it. I extract the following version of this story from a note in Vol. I. of Prescott's admired 'History of the Reign of Ferdinand and Isabella.' " *The Peña de los Enamorados* received its name from a tragical incident in Moorish history. A Christian slave succeeded in inspiring the daughter of his master, a wealthy Mussulman of Granada, with a passion for himself. The two lovers, after some time, fearful of the detection of their intrigue, resolved to make their escape into the Spanish territory. Before they could effect their purpose, however, they were hotly pursued by the damsel's father at the head of a party of Moorish horsemen, and overtaken near a precipice which rises between Archidona and Antequera. The unfortunate fugitives, who had scrambled to the summit of the rocks, finding all further escape impracticable, after tenderly embracing each other, threw themselves headlong from the dizzy heights, preferring this dreadful death to falling into the hands of their vindictive pursuers. The spot consecrated as the scene of the tragic incident has received the name of *Rock of the Lovers.*" Southey in his poem on the sad catastrophe, calls the youth Manuel, and the maiden Laila; but whether he professed to have any authority for so naming them, I am unable to say, and I have no leisure just now to make the inquiry.

At Granada we took up our abode at the *Fonda de los Siete Suelos,* an excellent hotel close to the Alhambra, and called after the *Torre de los Siete Suelos,* which nearly touches it on one side. From a door in this tower the unfortunate Boabdil, *El Rey chiquito,* sallied out with his belongings after the conquest of Granada. The situation of the hotel is delightful, cool, shady, and quiet, and we spent some very pleasant days there.

The town of Granada itself, now much fallen away from its former magnificence, will not be found particularly inviting to the mere sightseer. The streets, though often abounding in picturesque details and bright colouring, are for the most part narrow, irregular, and ill-paved; and one misses the charming *patios* of Seville and Cordova; only a few in comparison are to be seen here. But the markets for fruit, vegetables, and earthenware, are, as usual in Spanish towns, an attractive feature, and the public walks on the banks of the rivers Darro and Genil are cool, shady, and delicious.

The cathedral is a fine example of the so-called Græco-Roman style, and the effect inside is undoubtedly impressive. But lovers of Gothic architecture will not care to linger long in this cathedral, especially if they have already seen such churches as those at Burgos, Toledo, and Seville. There are, however, some good pictures to be seen in the building by the famous Alonzo Cano, his pupil Bocanegra, Ribera, and other artists.

I regret to say we missed seeing the " *Capilla de los Reyes,*" where are the tombs of Ferdinand and Isabella, and of their crazy daughter Joanna, and her handsome husband, Philip of Burgundy. How this sin of omission on our part came to be perpetrated I do not now remember, but it is our fixed determination to make due amends for it as soon as we shall be permitted to pay another visit to Granada.

But the far-famed Alhambra is, I need hardly say, the great point of interest in Granada. Not only is the ruined fortress, of which the palace forms a part, so interesting in itself, but the situation is most imposing, and the views from it at various points are truly magnificent.

From the *Fonda de los Siete Suelos* a short walk through the grove of elm trees brings you to the principal entrance to the fortress, *La Torre de Justicia*, the "Gate of Justice," a fine square, massive monument, so called because the Moorish kings were in the habit of settling disputes and dispensing judgment beneath it. Like Solomon and other Eastern potentates, "they made them porches where they might judge, even porches of judgment." Over the first arch of the gate a hand is sculptured with the fingers pointing upwards;

over the second arch a key is sculptured in like manner. Various interpretations have been given of this symbol. Popular tradition in the time of the Moors said that only when the hand grasped the key to open the gate, could the Christians enter into Granada. The hand, however, has not yet thought proper to lay hold of the key, but the Christians nevertheless entered Granada nearly 400 years ago, and have remained in possession ever since. It is a pity perhaps that the Moors were ever expelled from the country, but lamentations will not alter history, and we may console ourselves with the reflection that Spain still preserves a considerable allowance of that " Arabian spice" with which she was once so strongly impregnated.

That the gate was intended for defence as well as for a " porch of judgment" seems evident from its structure, and also from the inscription, " May God make this a protecting bulwark," which it bears. A narrow tortuous passage leads up through it to the great *Plaza de los Algibes,* or Place of the Cisterns, part of the walled-in terrace on which the Alhambra stands. On the left stand the ruins of the

Alcazaba, or citadel of the Moors, with its walls
and towers. On the other side gardens are
laid out, and the palace of Charles V. is seen,
beyond which are a church, a village, and other
buildings, all within the walls of the fortress.

The entrance to the Alhambra proper is
behind the palace of Charles V., down an
obscure alley. The exterior is absolutely insignificant, and was purposely made so, in
order to guard against the three greatest
enemies of the Moors, viz. heat, the evil eye,
and the enemy's projectile. You are thus in
no way prepared for the splendours which
await you within. We wandered in amaze-
ment through the marvellous halls and courts
which succeed one another in ever-varied
though harmonious beauty of decoration.
What the palace must have been when inhabited by the swarthy Moors and their dark-
eyed sultanas, one can only conjecture. Its
courts and halls are now bare and deserted,
and we can only people it in imagination with
inhabitants robed in gorgeous garments of silk
and fine linen, decorated with costly jewels,
and picture it furnished with rich hangings,
carpets, couches, and pillows, and perfumed

with all the fragrant odours of the East. In
order to form an adequate idea of what this
delightful abode must once have been like,
one must read over again some of the most
highly coloured descriptions in the 'Arabian
Nights.' "Pas plus que la Mosquée de Cor-
doue," says M. Robida truly, "l'Alhambra
de Grenade ne peut se décrire. On peut à
peine raconter comme le vague souvenir d'un
rêve, les promenades faites sous les galeries de
ses patios. On a rêvé. C'est trop beau pour
être vrai. L'Alhambra existe-t-il réellement?
Ne s'est on pas endormi sur les mille et une
nuits et n'a-t-on pas tout simplement rêvé ces
arcades fabuleusement découpées, ces patios
frais et ombreux d'un côté, étincelants de
l'autre, ces salles fantastiques, immenses,
obscures, où l'œil distingue à peine des orne-
ments pailletés, aux enroulements infinis, ces
jardins remplis d'orangers et habités unique-
ment par le souvenir des sultanes Mauresques,
de la légendaire Lindaraja?"*

Vandalism, neglect, and whitewash have
done their best to obscure the past. Charles V.
assisted in the work of destruction by pulling

* 'Les Vieilles Villes d'Espagne'—a charming book, beautifully illustrated.

down the greater part of the Moorish winter palace, and building up the modern palace before referred to in its place, which, however, for some reason or other, was never finished. This uncompleted palace is a fine building in itself, but utterly out of keeping with its surroundings. It is peculiar, moreover, in being square on the outside, while the interior is round like a bull-ring. The French, too, blew up as much as they could of what was left over and above from the devastation caused by those who had possession of the place before it fell into their hands in 1810–12. It passes comprehension what pleasure men can take in destroying these wonderful erections of bygone skill and magnificence. But man seems to be an incorrigibly destructive animal. Nothing at times is sacred from his fury and ignorance.

After visiting the inside of the palace, we went up one of the towers, from which the whole country round and the town beneath can be seen. I never beheld so magnificent a view. In front, beyond the city, lies the beautiful plain,

> " *Fresca y regalada vega,*
> *Dulce recreacion de damas,*
> *Y de hombres gloria immensa,*"

bounded by ranges of mountains. Behind, the
snow-clad Sierra Nevada rises majestically.
From here you see the *Generalife* (the country
palace of the Moorish kings), the Cartuja
convent, and San Miguel—the two latter
being on the opposite side of the river
Darro, on the hill, where are also remains of
old Moorish walls, quaint houses with wonderful balconies, and caves inhabited by
gitanos; and then such a sky to light it all up.
It is quite beyond my powers to describe the
enchantment of the whole scene—

> " A scene where, if a god should cast his sight,
> A god might gaze and wander with delight."

The *Generalife* is divided from the Alhambra
by a deep and romantic ravine. Of the
ancient building called by this name a few
impaired remains are all that are now left to
testify, with a sad kind of eloquence, to the
former splendour of this once favourite summer
abode of the Moorish sovereigns. The most
interesting parts still remaining are the
charming gallery at the end of the garden
first entered, from the arched windows in
which another enchanting panorama spreads
itself out before you. Beneath, from a fresh

point of view, are seen the city, as if reclining on a soft bed of flowers, the incomparable *Vega*, the winding river, pleasant country villas, or *cármencs*, as they are called in Granada, with their gardens and lanes of cypresses and myrtle. On the left stands the fortress of the Alhambra, with its venerable walls and square, stern-looking towers. Close by are the remains of the *Mihrab*, or sanctuary, whose arch is adorned with lace-like ornamentation and arabesque designs, with the inscription, " *God is great*," frequently repeated. Opposite, on the other side of the gardens, is a delightful rustic arbour, and in the centre of the court of the palace is a pond overshadowed by laurels and jessamine.

In a hall in the palace are shown some smoky-looking portraits of Moorish kings, devoid of artistic merit, and only historically interesting ; among others those of Abu Ali Hassan or Muley Abol-Hacen, father of poor Boabdil, and of that unlucky monarch himself, whose real name was Abo-Abdil-lah *el Zoyoíbi*, &c., &c.

But the real charm of the *Generalife* consists in its delightful gardens, with their trans-

parent pools and trickling fountains, so sug-
gestive of refreshing coolness during intense
summer heats, and over and above all "*cette
senteur d'Arabie restée flottante dans l'air*," as
the elder Dumas has so aptly expressed it.
Under one of the most venerable of the trees
in the garden a scene *à la Watteau* is allege l
to have been enacted between the Sultana
Zoraya and her lover, who belonged to the
noble family of the Abencerrages. The tree
was pointed out to us, but there are, I believe,
good reasons for doubting the authenticity of
the story, which appears to have been invented,
with other equally false charges, by one of the
Zegri family, in order to ruin their enemies
the Abencerrages.

An avenue of tall cypresses leads up to this
charming abode. We were told a "permission" was necessary to see the place, but
omitted nevertheless to provide one. We
were asked for it by the porter, who at first
seemed inclined to deny us admission; but on
my assuming a supplicating aspect and cere-
moniously producing our passport, we were
allowed in and shown everything. The gar-
dener expects a trifle for opening the gate of

the avenue and bowing you out. But a little will satisfy him, and if you are a lady he will give you a nice nosegay of flowers. The old gentleman who took us up to the top of the tower of the Alhambra, from which we saw the first of the fine panoramas above mentioned, was extra polite in this way, and produced the best flowers he could find in his little garden. These men are not extortionate. If you ask them beforehand what there is to pay for their services, the answer generally is " *Nada* " (nothing), or " *Es à voluntad* " (What you please, sir).

One afternoon we took a carriage down to the Cartuja convent, which lies a little way outside the town. It contains some indifferent pictures of martyrdoms and persecutions, inflicted, as is alleged, on Carthusians by English Protestants, and some gorgeous decorations in marble.

Comparatively few traces of the Moor remain in the town of Granada itself. Vestiges of the *Alcaiceria*, the Moors' silk bazaar, are still to be seen near the principal Moorish street, *El Zacatin*, and are well worthy of a visit.

The famous square of *Bivarambla*, formerly the scene of many jousts, tournaments, and suchlike deeds of chivalry, is now the *Plaza de la Constitucion.* Near it was the Gate Bibalraml, the Gate of the River, towards which the old Moorish king was riding when the news of the fall of Alhama reached him. So says the melancholy old romance, '*Passeavase el Rey Moro,*' &c., composed to commemorate the sad event. Lord Byron's version of this ballad is of course well known.

This was the first conquest in the memorable war of Granada, and the report of the disaster, says Prescott, " fell like the knell of their own doom on the ears of the inhabitants of the city." The woeful ballad gave expression to the depressed feelings of the people, so much so, that it was not allowed to be sung by the Moors on pain of death after the conquest.

We were rather afraid of penetrating into the haunts of the gipsies on the *Monte-Sacro*, for the tricks of these gentry are sometimes disagreeable, and their begging and pilfering propensities are notorious. We saw, however, some stray specimens of this peculiar people. A very handsome, dark-eyed *Gitano* haunted the doors of our hotel. He was dressed in the most approved brigand costume, and wore altogether a formidable aspect. He offered his services to me as guide, which, in fear and trembling, I declined. Sometimes you will see him plunge his hand into the pocket of his jacket, from which you expect he will produce either a revolver or a knife, and stretch your body lifeless on the ground. But he has no such bloodthirsty object in view, and instead of a deadly weapon he only takes out a photograph of himself, which he asks you to buy. His face is undoubtedly his fortune, for he was the model chosen by the painter, Fortuny, during his stay at Granada, and since the death of the artist he gains his livelihood by selling his portrait to strangers. When not so employed he spends his time in religiously doing nothing, after the manner of his race.

CHAPTER VII.

As Spain is still more the land of the past than the present, a tour there would, we thought, be hardly complete without a journey by one of the old-fashioned diligences. One, or rather two, run daily between Granada and Menjibar, a station on the railway to Madrid, to which latter place we were now obliged to retrace our steps. We could have gone the whole way by rail, but this would have involved a long round by way of Cordova, where we had already been, whereas the journey by road was considerably shorter as regards distance, and did not, moreover, take up so much time. We decided, therefore, in favour of the diligence as far as Menjibar, and took places accordingly.

The vehicle started at five o'clock in the morning from the *Plaza de la Constitucion,* so

we had to be up betimes. We had secured
two places in the *berlina* (or *coupé* in French),
and were so fortunate as to have it all to
ourselves the whole way, although it was
intended to hold three persons. Our conveyance was not a very brilliant specimen of its
class. It was drawn during the first stage by
a mixed team of horses and mules, sometimes
three, sometimes four in number. They were
tolerably respectable animals, and the road
being excellent, we went along at a good
pace. The driver (*mayoral*) was a very
cheery individual, and kept shouting to his
quadrupeds almost the whole way. The first
part of the journey was performed in darkness, and the morning air was chilly. Our
spirits were somewhat depressed in consequence. But when the sun rose we got
gradually warmer and more comfortable, and
were enabled to divert our minds with the
sight of the country through which we were
passing; and very grand it was most of the
way. Our route lay through some fine rocky
hills and valleys, and along rapid rivers.
Part of the way was very winding, and there
were consequently frequent varieties in the

landscape. The scenery is decidedly interesting, at least as far as Jaen.

We changed quadrupeds several times, once in a poor-looking, beggarly village, called, if I remember rightly, Campilo, once in Jaen, and the other times near solitary houses or inns (*ventas*) by the roadside.

Jaen is the only town of importance through which we passed. It is beautifully situated. The Romans called it *Aurinx*, or *Oringis*. It was in their time, and is still, as Livy says, " a desirable spot, the adjacent parts affording mines of silver, and the soil being fruitful." It was, at the time of which he writes, in the hands of the Carthaginians, and "the place served Hasdrubal as a fortress, whence he used to make incursions on the states around."* It was besieged and taken by Lucius Scipio, who was sent by his brother with an army of 10,000 foot and 1000 horse for that purpose.

The traces of Roman rule in Jaen, as well as of Moorish, which latter lasted for five centuries, have been almost entirely swept away, as has been the case in many other

* See Livy, bk. xxviii. chap. iii., Baker's translation.

towns in Spain. But Jaen is interesting still nevertheless. It possesses a fine cathedral, built in the first part of the sixteenth century on the ruins of a former church erected by St. Ferdinand on the site of a great Moorish mosque. There are also picturesque remains of an old castle on the slope of the hill overlooking the town. We had a fine view of the whole town, with the cathedral rising in the middle, and the old castle in the background, just before arriving.

I only regret we had not time to explore the place a little more at leisure, but our short halt only allowed us time to attend to the cravings of the inner man, which had for some time been unceremoniously asserting themselves. So true is it that

> " Nothing more shameless is than appetite,
> Who still, whatever anguish load our breast,
> Makes us remember, in our own despite,
> Both food and drink."

Instead, therefore, of going in search of objects of art and antiquity, we repaired to the *Fonda Europa*—the best inn in the town —with a view to procuring some light refreshment. It was a tidy-looking place enough, and a comely damsel received us, and showed us into a small, but comfortable coffee-room, where a table was laid for dinner. We ordered fried eggs and coffee, which were so long in making their appearance that we began to think the people of the inn must have had a design to make us miss our conveyance, and spend the night at their establishment. They failed, however, in their intention, if, indeed, they had any such; for by dint of a little fussing we succeeded in making them produce what we had asked for. The eggs were good, but were spoiled by being fried in very nasty oil. The coffee was good and refreshing. I have purposely forgotten what the charge was, as I suspect the waiter took advantage of our hurry to be off, and imposed upon us; if so, it was one of the few instances of extortion I can call to mind during our stay in Spain.

We now not only changed our team, but our diligence, and were provided with a much more imposing vehicle, drawn by eight animals, with a postilion (*delantero*) on one of the leaders. This was the last stage, and much the most uninteresting. The country was dreary, and the road dusty, so we shut up the windows (which were made, not of glass, be it known, but of wood), and wished for Menjibar. We eventually arrived there soon after five o'clock in the afternoon, having been twelve hours on the road. A good dinner at the buffet at the railway station soon made us forget the not very serious fatigue we had undergone. We had not long finished our repast when the Madrid train arrived. We reached that city next morning at six o'clock, and were not sorry to get to our hotel, although we were really none the worse for our twenty-six hours' journey. Our luggage was registered the whole way from Granada to Madrid.

This time we chose the *Hotel de Paris*, on the *Puerta del Sol*, which is certainly preferable to the *Embajadores*, although perhaps a little dearer.

We had hoped when in Madrid before to have been able to see the famous armoury, but it was closed for cleaning on the day we applied for admission. This time we tried again, but also without success; the place was shut on account of the inclemency of the weather. It is an odd fashion which prevails in Madrid to *close* museums and picture galleries on wet days. One would imagine that exhibitions of this kind ought rather to be open on such days, in order to provide rational diversion for the people when they cannot so well take their pleasure in the open air. But they manage things differently in Spain.

Bull-fights are announced to take place only *si el tiempo lo permite,* which is reasonable enough, as they are, so far as the actors and a great part of the spectators are concerned, open-air entertainments. If, however, the rain begins, as was the case when we were present, after the *funcion* has commenced, there is no power to stop the performance. It is then too late to disappoint the excited crowd. But it is obviously otherwise with museums and picture galleries, which are of course always under cover.

CHAPTER VIII.

ALCALÁ-ZARAGOZA.

"Then Zaragoza—blighted be the tongue
That names thy name without the honour due."
Scott's *Vision of Don Roderick.*

On Saturday we left Madrid for Zaragoza. Learning from that useful compilation ' Bradshaw,' that " the scenery along this line is very interesting, the railway traversing two ranges of rocky mountains," we chose the morning train, which leaves Madrid at 7·5 A.M., in preference to the night one, leaving at 7.30 P.M., although the latter train is much the quicker of the two.

The route traversed is not interesting just at first, but it becomes more and more so as you go along. The mountains have much the same character as those we have already seen, being chiefly remarkable for ruggedness and wild grandeur. Unfortunately darkness set in before we arrived at our destination, so that we missed seeing a good deal of the country through which the latter part of our route lay.

All the principal towns along the line are full of interesting associations, and fortunately good general views of them are to be had from the train. We stopped at every station, and crept along so slowly that we had plenty of time to look about us. The first place of importance is Alcalá de Henares, the seat of Cardinal Ximenes de Cisneros' once celebrated, but now decayed, university. Here too Ximenes published his famous Bible, called the Complutensian Polyglot, from Complutum, the old Roman name of the place, a work which was only brought to an end in 1517, a few months before his death, fifteen years after its commencement, and which is said to have cost him 80,000 golden crowns. He had types cast for the purpose in his own foundries at Alcalá, and he imported artists from Germany to execute the work. A perfect copy of this, the first Polyglot Bible, was disposed of in the sale of the Sunderland Library for the sum of 195*l.* Although the illustrious cardinal occupied so commanding a position in the two somewhat dissimilar, and occasionally conflicting, spheres of religion and politics, his wardrobe would appear to have been of a very limited nature; and it was, we are driven to conclude, totally unprovided with an article now generally considered as of prime necessity, viz. *linen.* "He commonly slept in his Franciscan habit. Of course, his toilet took no long time. On one occasion when he was travelling, and up as usual long before dawn, he urged his muleteer to dress himself quickly, at which the latter irreverently exclaimed, ' *Cuerpo de Dios!* does your holiness think I have nothing more to do than to shake myself like a wet spaniel, and tighten my cord a little.' " *

At Alcalá were born Doña Catalina, the youngest child of Ferdinand and Isabella, better known in English history as Catherine of Arragon, Ferdinand, afterwards Emperor of Germany, and the famous Cervantes, who also studied at the university before he removed to Salamanca. As in the case of Homer, several cities, including Toledo, Seville, and Madrid, contended for the honour of being the birthplace of the illustrious author; but

* Prescott.

their pretensions have now been set aside in favour of Alcalá.

Guadalajara is another interesting old place on the route, as are also Siguenza and Calatayud.

Siguenza, built on the slopes of a gently rising eminence, with its substantial walls, gates, and turrets, and an imposing old castle, has an air of compactness and strength about it as seen from the railway. It possesses, moreover, a striking cathedral, remarkable, among other things, for a beautiful rose window. The massive grandeur of this noble building, says Mr. Street somewhat despairingly, "is only a matter of envy to a wretched architect in the nineteenth century, whose main triumph, if he would prosper, must be to use as few bricks and as small fragments of stone as he can, to the intent that his work should certainly be cheap, and in forgetfulness, if possible, that it will also certainly be bad." The date of the foundation of this interesting edifice is uncertain, but it appears to have been restored by the king Don Alfonso VI., after he had succeeded in wresting Siguenza, Toledo, and Medinaceli from their former masters, the Moors. It is said to have been dedicated on the 19th June, 1102. The Frenchman, Don Bernardo, a monk of Cluny, was the first bishop of the see.

It will be remembered that the *learned* curate with whom Don Quixote used to dispute as to who was the better knight, Palmerin of England or Amadis de Gaul, is represented as having taken his degree at Siguenza. But this must be a bit of playful irony on the part of Cervantes, for it does not appear that Siguenza ever possessed a university at which the curate could have graduated. At all events it was only a very second-rate seat of learning. The two great universities of Spain were at Salamanca and Alcalá.*

Calatayud is the next city in importance in

---

* "The universities of Spain are now ten: Madrid, with 6672 students; Barcelona, with 2459; Valencia, 2118; Seville, 1382; Granada, 1225; Valladolid, 880; Santiago de Compostella, 779; Zaragoza, 771; Salamanca, 372; and Oviedo with 216; making a total of 16,874 university students. The number of regular professors is 415, with 240 supernumeraries and assistants, making a total of 655; that is, one professor to every 26 students. The salary of the professors varies from 120*l.* to 260*l.* per annum, except in Madrid, where it is from 160*l.* to 300*l.* The budget of the whole universities is a little over 1,000,000*l.*, and the expenditure slightly in excess, leaving a deficit in 1879 of 4600*l.* The average cost of each student to the university is a little over 6*l.*"—From the Rev. Wentworth Webster's ' Spain,' a book containing much useful and reliable information.

Arragon after Zaragoza, and is finely situated on rocky ground. Excavations in the rocks exist here, similar to those at Granada, where the poorer classes live in picturesque squalor. These dwellings are said to date from the time of the Moors.

The dress of the Arragonese peasantry now attracted our attention from its peculiarity, and because of its unlikeness to anything we had yet seen. The men as a rule wear no hats, but have instead a coloured handkerchief wound round the head, leaving the top quite bare. They wear knee-breeches slashed down the sides, and tied by strings below the knee, and an open waistcoat. Round the waist they wind a wide sash, which is made to act as a receptacle for articles of various kinds. Here are stowed away pipes, tobacco, money, provisions, and other odds and ends—the folds of the sash keeping everything as safe as a pocket. They also frequently carry a blanket of various colours, which they throw in a graceful manner over their shoulders. On their feet they wear a kind of sandal. The women's dress is not so remarkable as the men's, and need not be described particularly.

The weather was dismal and unfavourable during our stay at Zaragoza, which added to the natural gloom and sternness of the old Arragonese capital. The streets are narrow and ill-paved, and they were, at the time of our visit, very muddy in consequence of the rain which had recently fallen. The walk by the river-side was almost impassable on account of the mud and filth. We managed, however, to see the most of what was to be seen notwithstanding.

Zaragoza has two cathedrals, the older one, *La Seo*, the see, being much the more interesting. It still preserves a few traces of the Moorish period, notably on the exterior at the north-east angle of the church, where are some beautiful specimens of Moorish brick-work inlaid with tiles of various sizes, shapes, and colours. The interior is not very imposing, but there is still much to admire. Not the least remarkable part of the church is the pavement, which is a reproduction of the tracery of the roof. It is said to be the work of a Moorish artist, and to date from 1432.

The most curious monument in Zaragoza

is the *Torre Nueva*, a tall octagonal tower, which stands by itself, and inclines a little, like the tower at Pisa, only not so much. It is built of brick in remarkable patterns, after Moorish designs, and dates from about 1504. Although it has not long since been propped up on one side, in order to prevent a further deviation from the perpendicular, it looks as if it might topple over at any time. But it is in all probability safe enough. It is possible to go up to the top of it, from whence an extensive view of the surrounding country is doubtless to be had. But having no great curiosity to ascend, we preferred remaining on *terra firma*.

Not far from the tower is the picturesque old market-place. There is an old world, tumble-down appearance about the houses in this *Plaza* which is truly fascinating, and even seems to extend to the fruit and vegetable sellers who frequent it. They look as if they had been buried and dug up again. The day, however, being Sunday, there was not very much doing.

There was a performance in the afternoon at one of the theatres, to which I went. I came in for the two last acts of a melodrama, which did not appear to possess any very great merit. The acting, however, was fairly good. Then came what I went purposely to see, a *Baile Nacional*, i. e., some Spanish national dances. I never saw so good a ballet anywhere. It was quite a different sort of performance to the one seen by M. Théophile Gautier at Vitoria, and described in his 'Voyage en Espagne.' That, however, was forty years ago. The performers in this ballet, both male and female, danced most artistically, and none of them looked scraggy or worn out. The dances were beautifully arranged, and the dresses and scenery pretty and appropriate. There was, moreover, a total absence of those extravagant terpsichorean gymnastics which are so prevalent on other stages. The movements of the dancers were graceful rather than outlandish. The music, though by no means elaborate, was characteristic, and was played with perfect precision by a small, but quite efficient orchestra. It would pay, I should imagine, to import such a troupe bodily into England. The salaries of the performers must be very low, as the charges for admission were ludicrously cheap. I was seated in a most comfortable stall (*butaca*), for which I paid less than two shillings in English money.

Our tour in Spain No. 1, which had been such a source of pleasure to us, and I hope of profit too, was now virtually at an end. Our time was nearly up, and we had to return to England. We left Zaragoza in the evening in pelting rain, and reached Bayonne by the ordinary route next day. It is impossible to help noticing the remarkable contrast between the two places, the one bright, clean, and pleasant, the other stern and dismal. An air of prosperity and progress pervades the latter town, but is conspicuously absent from the former. There is, however, I believe, a certain amount of business doing in Zaragoza, chiefly, I was told, in the wine trade. But one does not go to Spain in search of signs of commercial activity. In most of the old towns such a commonplace thing as *business*, in the modern acceptation of the term, is but little understood. "Great rest standeth in little business" would appear to be their favourite motto. In one sense, of course, this is to be regretted. But even commerce is not without its drawbacks, and it is, it must be owned, by no means generally favourable to the preservation of picturesqueness and local colour. If you have a taste for antiquities and old historical associations Spain will be a place after your own heart; but if, on the other hand, you hold that "the age of ruins is past," you will be a fish out of water there, and you will be more in your element in Manchester.

CHAPTER IX.

In the beginning of September in the following year we set out for Spain again, entering it this time by way of Lyons, Dijon, Avignon, Nimes, Montpellier, and Perpignan, and so on to the frontier between Cerbère and Port Bon.

In Paris we provided ourselves with circular tickets to take us down as far as Valencia and back by Madrid, Irun, and Bordeaux. The advantages conferred by these tickets are many and great. A very considerable saving of expense and likewise trouble is effected, and you are allowed to travel by any train, and to stop when and where you choose; but you are, of course, tied to your route, and are limited as to time, which, however, we found amply sufficient. You can start either from the Orleans railway station, and go by Bordeaux, &c., or from the Lyons station, and go by Dijon and Clermont; but once started you must stick to the route marked out for you. The tickets are to be had at either the Orleans or Lyons railway stations, or at the Bureau Central, 130, Rue St. Honoré, where full particulars can be obtained.

We stopped a couple of nights at Avignon in order to explore the antiquities of that charming old town. The streets, for the most part narrow and tortuous, still preserve a medieval appearance. In the summer they are covered with canvas, as in Spain, to keep out the heat. Indeed, Avignon has more the appearance of a Spanish or an Italian than a French town. The colossal papal palace, the residence in the fourteenth century of seven popes and two anti-popes, is alas! a palace no longer, but is used for the commonplace purposes of a barrack. The halls have been altered for the convenience of the military, the frescoes which decorated the walls have been nearly all demolished, and, with the exception of a few on the south side, the windows, which in former days were small, narrow, and pointed, have been changed into unmeaning ugly square openings. The restoration of the palace from designs by M. Viollet-le-Duc, and its ·evacuation by the military, have been proposed ; but unluckily the project has fallen through. From the promenade on the platform of the *Rocher des Doms,* near the cathedral and adjoining palace, we had a view which reminded us not a little of the *vega* of Granada as seen from the towers of the Alhambra, and the *Mirador* of the *Generalife.*

The ramparts surrounding the town exist nearly in their original state, and are an excellent specimen of the style of fortification in vogue in the fourteenth century.

We looked into most of the churches, and also into the museum, which contains some valuable Roman remains found in the locality, and not a few respectable pictures. The tomb of Petrarch's Laura, once in the Church des Cordeliers, is no longer to be seen. A modest cross erected in 1823 by the Englishman, Mr. Charles Kelsall, which used to mark the spot, is now in the garden of the museum.

A new line of railway, which has been

open about a year, runs on the right bank
of the Rhone from Lyons to Nimes. We
started by it from the Pont d'Avignon
station, near the once important suburb of
Villeneuve les Avignon, on our way to
Nimes and Montpellier, stopping at the
Remoulins station, whence we drove out to
the famous *Pont du Gard*, about a mile and a
half away. It is quite easy to climb up into
this stupendous monument of antiquity by
means of a spiral staircase which has been
constructed at one of the ends, and you can
walk across it through the channel lined with
cement, now hardened by time, and covered
by large flat stones, which conducted the
water from the fountains of Eure and Airan,
near Uzès, to Nimes, more than 1800 years
ago.

We did our best in the few hours at our
disposal to explore the wonders of Nimes,
and we have carried away, I hope, a tolerably
fair impression of the great amphitheatre, the
Maison Carrée, the so-called Temple of Diana,
the Tour Magne, &c., &c., which some good
photographs purchased on the spot will help
to revive.

There is little to be seen at Montpellier except the admirable Musée Fabre, containing the picture gallery, which should on no account be missed, as it possesses some first-rate examples of Dutch artists, viz.:—Gerard Dow (La Souricière), Metzu, D. Teniers, Steen, &c., besides works by masters of other schools, such as a *Sainte Marie Egyptienne*, by Ribera, firmly painted, but not pleasing, an Angel Gabriel and Sta. Agatha by Zurbaran, and last, not least, the *Infant Samuel*, by Sir Joshua Reynolds, the only picture by that painter as yet possessed by France.

Perpignan is not much frequented by travellers, but it is worth a visit on account of its remarkable citadel, begun by the kings of Arragon, when this part of France belonged to Spain, and afterwards strengthened by Charles V., and its quaint Spanish-looking streets and houses. The cathedral, too, with its broad single nave is not to be overlooked, nor the old Lonja, or exchange, now used as a café. The promenades also round the town are very pleasant, and were crowded with a motley throng on the afternoon of the Sunday we spent there.

I

Our steps were directed in the first instance to Barcelona. The country we passed through on our way there is quite beautiful, in parts rocky and precipitous, with here and there glimpses of the dark blue waters of the Mediterranean. Vines, olives, and maize grow in abundance, and good cultivation combined with irrigation seemed the rule. The people everywhere were busy gathering the grapes. Groups of peasants were to be seen in every vineyard hard at work, the men in blue blouses and long red nightcap-shaped *gorros*, and the women with large wide-brimmed hats on their heads to shade them from the sun. The grapes were being taken out of the vineyards in cartloads.

Gerona is the first place of any importance on the line. This interesting old town, famous in history on account of the obstinate bravery displayed by its inhabitants during the numerous sieges it has sustained, enjoys the advantage of a fine situation on the banks of the river Oña. Quaint houses overlook the banks of the river, and their balconies adorned with many-coloured hangings have a bright and pleasing effect. The fine cathedral rises on an eminence about the centre of the town, and near it is the *Collegiata* of San Felice, surmounted by a lofty tower.

We also passed Hostalrich, another most remarkable place, a little further on, strongly fortified with a citadel, ramparts, and ancient towers. Windows have been constructed in the old walls, giving light to dwellings behind—a singular arrangement, the like of which is, I should think, hardly to be seen anywhere else. The importance derived by this fortress, both from its natural position and from the strength of its fortifications, has caused it to figure conspicuously in many a contest between the French and Spaniards. Nor has it been behindhand in playing its part in the civil revolts which from time to time have agitated Catalonia. Unfortunately the guide-books do not say much about this curious place.

Barcelona is full of life and movement, and the enterprising Catalonians have good reason to be proud of their prosperous city. The promenades are frequented late and early, especially the so-called *Rambla*, which divides the town into two nearly equal parts. It is

I 2

sheltered by fine trees on both sides, and is always shady and pleasant. There are several other promenades, however, and a beautiful new park and garden which have been laid out on the site of the ancient citadel. The town is rapidly growing in all directions, and now occupies about ten times the space of the old town. Well-built houses are being erected and new streets added every day. The new part (*the ensanche* as it is called) is laid out in squares, somewhat after the fashion of a chess-board.

Barcelona, however, is not all new by any means, and those who travel in search of the picturesque can gladden their hearts and gratify their cravings to any extent in the narrow, tortuous streets in the neighbourhood of the fine cathedral. Here they will find delightful balconies with hangings in various colours, and every now and then a little bit of verdure is added to the picture, while a bright blue sky sheds down its light from above.

There is some splendid stained glass in the cathedral, also some good carving in the choir. The interior of the church is very imposing, and the elegance and boldness of the graceful pillars supporting the vaulted roof very striking. The dark-brown colour of the stone of which the building is composed greatly heightens the general effect, imparting as it does a sombre tone to the whole edifice. We were present twice while mass was being celebrated, and heard some good organ-playing. The people were kneeling and standing about in groups, as is usual in Spanish cathedrals, the ladies with black mantillas and fans. The whole scene would have formed a most effective subject for a picture.

There are several other churches in Barcelona, the finest of which is perhaps the church of *Sta. Maria del Mar.*

Not far from the cathedral on the *Plaza de la Constitucion* is the *Casa de la Diputacion,* the oldest and best parts of which are the exquisite façade of the chapel of St. George in the *Calle del Obispo,* the grand staircase, and the galleries round the court of orange trees.

On the opposite side of the Plaza is the town hall (*Casas Consistoriales*), of which, however, there is little to interest remaining, except a charming side façade looking on to a little garden.

The guide-books misled us completely as to the whereabouts of the post-office, where we expected to find letters. They place it on the *Rambla*, not far from the sea, whereas it is now, whatever may have been the case formerly, in exactly the opposite direction, viz. on the *Plaza Cataluña*, at the extreme top of the *Rambla*.

Barcelona, in addition to its many other attractions, possesses by all accounts a most charming climate. The weather was brilliant while we were there, but it is said to be very mild as a rule. The mean temperature is about 60° (Fahr.), the heat in summer never exceeds 87° (Fahr.), and the cold is never below 28°. The mean temperature in winter is about 50°.

We next set out for Tarragona. The scenery along the route again for the most part interesting, especially as you approach Martorell. At the entrance to this town is the magnificent *Puente del Diablo*, or Devil's Bridge, consisting of an immense ogival-pointed arch, constructed in reddish stone. The bridge is very narrow and very steep. On the summit is a sort of portico, under which only foot-passengers and beasts of burden pass, for the bridge is too steep for vehicles. At the entrance as you approach the town is a triumphal arch of probably about the same age as the bridge itself, and very plain and massive. The foundation of the bridge is ascribed to Hannibal, and the triumphal arch is said to have been elevated in honour of Hamilcar. But the work here attributed to the Carthaginian is much more probably Roman. The wide centre arch as we now see it is the work of the Moors. This is one of the finest monuments of its kind in Spain, and the scenery of the neigh-bourhood is delightful. On your right as you pass along is a beautiful plain watered by the *Llobregat*, and every now and then you get glimpses of the immense serrated pyramid of the Montserrat, forming a worthy background to the landscape. Quaint villages are seen at intervals, with picturesque little churches and their towers, and an occasional castle, generally on the summit of a rock, and invariably in a ruinous state.

Tarragona will compare favourably with Toledo as regards situation, for it is built

on the summit of a limestone rock overlooking
the Mediterranean, and in some respects, at
least, it is little behind it as regards objects
of antiquarian interest. It would be almost
enough to mention the Cyclopean walls
founded by the Carthaginians, and built upon
by the Romans, in proof of this assertion.
It is impossible to look upon these huge
walls, composed of enormous stones, without
feelings of astonishment. One is perplexed
when one thinks of the labour it must have
cost to move such colossal masses, and put
them in their places. No one, in these
economical and degenerate days, would even
dream of taking the time or trouble necessary
to erect anything half so solid and immovable.

But there are, besides, various other monuments of the Roman epoch to be found in
Tarragona by those who diligently search
after them. I may mention, among others,
the *Castillo de Pilatos*, formerly the palace
of Augustus, the *Puerta de San Antonio*, &c.
In the upper part of the town many of the
houses have been built with the stones and
other materials taken from the ruins of Roman

palaces and buildings. We met with several slabs with Roman inscriptions, built into the walls, especially in the *Calle de la Merceria,* close to the cathedral.

The *Calle Major,* which leads up towards the cathedral, is a steep, irregular street, full of character and colour.

You approach the principal *façade* of the cathedral by a flight of steps, as is usual in Catalonia. It consists of a fine deeply recessed portal, flanked by two square piers, crowned by pinnacles. Above the door is a beautiful rose window. The interior is vast and majestic, but decidedly heavy, and contrasts in this respect unfavourably with the lightness and boldness of the interior of the cathedral at Barcelona. This was, at all events, the effect produced upon me. More competent judges, however, such as Street, look upon this church as one of the noblest and most interesting in Spain, " producing in a very marked degree an extremely impressive internal effect, without being on an exaggerated scale, and combining in the happiest fashion the greatest solidity of construction with a lavish display of ornament in some parts, to which it is hard to find a parallel."

The ordinary visitor, however, will probably consider the cloisters the most interesting part of the edifice. I will not presume to enter into technical details, which are to be found better given elsewhere, but merely describe them as supremely beautiful. In the centre is a charming court open to the blue sky, where various flowering shrubs grow in profusion, including the plumbago and oleander (the *laurier rose*, the sight of which invariably filled M. Théophile Gautier with ecstasies).

The comical enters largely into the sculpturing of the abaci of some of the capitals in this cloister. It is impossible to help laughing at the story of the cat and the rats, or mice, whichever you like, represented on one of them; it is so full of life and humour. The apparently lifeless body of the cat is borne along in solemn procession, when all of a sudden the wily animal jumps up and puts her undertakers to flight in all directions. They had foolishly forgotten to tie her legs before placing her on the hearse.

There is a curious little church behind the cathedral called *San Pablo,* said to have been built by St. Paul,

> " *Credat Judæus Apella;*
> *Non ego* " :

for it is quite uncertain whether the great Apostle of the Gentiles ever was in Spain, much less that he built a church there; and although he tells the Christians at Rome that he intended to " go on by them into Spain," there is no reliable evidence to show that he ever accomplished his purpose. In those days, be it remembered, circular tickets and other facilities were not in general use for the convenience of tourists. In any case, however, the church is decidedly old, and it has a quaint little *façade* which is well worth inspection.

CHAPTER X.

VALENCIA—SAGUNTUM.

THE finest scenery between Tarragona and Valencia is near Tortosa, an important military position with strong fortifications. It is on the Ebro, and the products of Arragon and Navarre, such as, oil, corn, wood, and wine, are brought down here by the river in large quantities.

The first thing we did, on the morning after our arrival at Valencia, was to engage a vehicle for a drive through the principal streets, promenades, &c., in order to obtain a good general view of this "Sultana of Mediterranean cities." Valencia is well provided with public conveyances, and the horses attached to them are excellent. The most characteristic is the *tartana*, a covered vehicle on two wheels with springs, or what pretend to be such. The driver sits on a seat contrived in a peculiar fashion on the off shaft, with his feet resting on a small footboard made of iron. Neatly constructed small omnibuses are also popular, and there are open cabs as well.

The streets with their *miradores* and accompaniments are even more fascinating than those we had already seen in other towns in Spain, and the costumes of the dark oriental-looking peasantry give additional colour to the surroundings. The "people" are chiefly to be seen on the principal market-place (*mercado*), where a lively business in fruit and vegetable dealing is carried on in the mornings, and a confused Babel of tongues salutes your ears as you pass through. This market is indeed one of the most attractive sights in Valencia, for it is brim full of character and local colour well and judiciously laid on.

The fruit principally dealt in is the water-melon, which is, so to speak, meat, drink, lodging, and washing to the humble Valencianos. Its value as food, and even drink, will hardly be disputed, and it is currently reported that the Valencian peasant occasionally washes his face, at least, *if no more,* with the refreshing juice, using his many-coloured *manta* as a towel. Sir Henry Thompson, in his 'Food and Feeding,' is loud in praise of these water-melons, "which fill the mouth," as he justly says, "with cool fragrant liquid."

The interesting old *Lonja de Seda,* or silk exchange, is on one side of the *mercado.* The most remarkable part of this building is the fine hall, divided into three naves, the vaults being supported by bold and graceful spiral columns.

Strange to say, the buildings in Valencia, with the exception of the *Lonja,* are almost totally devoid of interest. The cathedral has but little to recommend it. The best parts are the octagonal steeple, called *El Miguelete,* or *Micalet,* in Valencian, from the name of its great bell, baptized with that appellation on the Feast of St. Michael, 1521; the great doors and the beautiful lantern, or *cimborio,* also octagonal, considered one of the finest examples of its class in Spain. The interior is modernised, heavy and unattractive, and but for the pictures contained therein would be hardly worth visiting.

The same may be said of the other numerous churches, many of which, especially *San Nicolas,* possess good pictures by the great Valencian painter, Juan Juanes, as well as by Ribera, Ribalta, Espinosa, &c. In one of the side chapels of the cathedral we noted a most beautiful Virgin by Sassoferrato. You go to Valencia to study Juanes, as you go to Seville for Murillo, and to Madrid for Velasquez. There are no doubt some great works by Juanes in the Madrid picture-gallery, notably the magnificent Last Supper, and the two pictures representing St. Stephen preaching. But at Valencia the examples are more numerous, and they are well worth careful inspection. For composition and finish, combined with beauty of colouring, it is difficult to imagine anything superior. A certain hardness, however, as it appears to me, is sometimes observable in the treatment; but the draperies are beautiful and exquisitely folded.

The museum at Valencia, although containing a vast amount of rubbish, has still some good specimens by the above painter, besides other works of the Valencian School. There is also a charming portrait of a lady by Goya, "all life, freshness, and españolismo," as my guide, philosopher, and friend, Mr. O'Shea, justly remarks. There is an indescribable "*chic*," as they say in France, about the attitude and expression of this fascinating personage, as she sits bolt upright on the trunk of a tree, with her mantilla and her fan. It is a great misfortune, I think, that so many of the pictures at Valencia are scattered about in the various churches, where they are often hidden away in the sacristies and other inaccessible places. If the sacristan is not in the way, you will often have to go away without seeing anything. How much better it would be to have all the pictures collected in a good gallery, well catalogued and arranged! But at present, at least, there seems no likelihood of this desirable end being brought about.

Of the old walls once encircling the city, with their gates at intervals, much is still left in a good state of preservation. The two finest gates are the *Puerta de Serranos*, on the road to Arragon and Catalonia, flanked on both sides of the entrance archway by two lofty polygonal towers, and the *Puerta de*

Cuarte, on the road to Madrid, flanked by
circular towers. The former gateway was
finished in 1381, and the latter in 1444.
Both are imposing, especially the *Puerta de
Serranos*. They are now used as prisons.

Many of the houses of the principal inhabitants are well worth a glance in passing,
especially those in the *Calle de Caballeros*, the
most aristocratic street. They are remarkable
for their solidity, and have often fine *patios*,
massive staircases with richly carved banisters,
and arched colonnades adorned with Gothic
and *ajimez* windows. Opposite to one of our
windows in the *Fonda Villa de Madrid* was
the rich but somewhat grotesquely sculptured
marble façade of the mansion of the Marques
de dos Aguas, considered one of the finest
private houses in Valencia.

We went up one morning to the top of the
cathedral tower, whence there is a most magnificent view of the town beneath, with its
remains of old walls and gates, and of the
rich garden of Valencia beyond. The most
distant objects could be distinctly seen through
the transparent atmosphere.

We are now in the headquarters of *Orcha-*

K

terias, where refreshing drinks, known as
Orchatas, are concocted, and imbibed by the
thirsty. The most common is the *Orchata de
chufas*, which is made from the milk of the
chufa, a sort of earth almond, the *Cyperus
esculentus* of Linnæus. There are, however,
several others. This industry, even in other
towns of Spain, is carried on exclusively by
natives of Valencia.

The public walks about Valencia are very
charming, especially the *Glorieta*, laid out
with palms and other tropical plants, where
the band plays in the summer on Sunday and
Thursday evenings, and the *Alameda*, on the
further side of the river, where Valencian
high life drives in the afternoons about six
o'clock.

But the most important event which
occurred during our sojourn at Valencia was
our expedition to ancient Saguntum.

Every schoolmaster and schoolboy knows
how that the inhabitants of Saguntum were
faithfully attached to the Romans, and how
they withstood a siege of eight months, more
or less, against Hannibal, till, urged by
famine, they heroically destroyed themselves

and their valuables in a general conflagration,
rather than fall into the hands of the enemy.
It is also well known how that the fall of the
place was the cause of the Second Punic War.
Add a few more facts, and a couple of fairly
well authenticated dates, and you will have
the dry bones of history complete, and much
good may they do you. But pay a visit to
Saguntum, and your historical dry bones will
live and move and have their being before
your very eyes. You will climb the citadel,
and see the old walls, portions of which remain
as they were originally in primitive Saguntine
times, although since added to by the various
masters of Spain. You will explore the
ancient theatre on the slope of the hill beneath
the citadel, said to be the best specimen in
existence. You can stand on the stage and
sit on the seats, still plainly to be seen and sat
upon, where the Saguntines of old sat and
witnessed the performances represented. By
this time you will have begun to realise what
history means when it talks about the siege of
Saguntum, the cause of the Second Punic War,
and so forth; and you will turn, when you
reach home, to the 21st book of your 'Titus

Livius' with as much avidity as the Baron of Bradwardine habitually showed for that eminent but somewhat untrustworthy historian.

We picked up an intelligent youth at the railway station, a bit of an antiquarian himself, who undertook to show us the way to the old ruins through the straggling modern town of Sagunto (called until recently Murviedro from *muri veteres*), and to procure the key of the enclosure of the theatre, which has been wisely walled in to prevent depredations.

The theatre is, as before stated, situated on the slope of the hill, as was usual in the case of ancient theatres. The position is superb, and the audience, if they found the play tedious, could enjoy the beautiful prospect over the fertile valley beneath, in all its essential features the same now as of old.* The situation was well chosen too in other ways, for it admitted only the refreshing breezes from the east, more welcome in that warm

---

* "They carefully made choice of a beautiful situation. The theatre of Tauromenium, at present Taormino, in Sicily, of which the ruins are still visible, was, according to Munter's description, situated in such a manner, that the audience had a view of Etna over the background of the theatre."—*Schlegel.*

climate than with us, and other winds, more likely to be injurious to health, were excluded.

The date of its foundation is uncertain. Some say it was erected by the Romans in the time of the Scipios, by their desire, and at the expense of the Roman treasury, in order to show their gratitude towards the Saguntines, their constant friends and allies. Others attribute its construction to the Emperor Claudius Germanicus, with a like intention. But others, again, consider that there are good grounds for believing that it existed before the Romans had possession of Spain, and that consequently its construction dates from the time of the Greek colonists.

Be this as it may, it is a marvellously interesting monument, and is admitted to be one of the best of its kind to be seen anywhere, Italy not excepted. All the principal arrangements of the ancient theatre can here be traced more or less distinctly, the *scenium*, *proscenium*, and orchestra, the withdrawing rooms for the actors, the receptacles for the stage machinery, and the entrances for the audience according to the different grades of persons usually composing it. We entered

the ruin at the back of the *proscenium*, through
a small round arched passage sloping upwards,
by means of which we emerged on to the
orchestra.   What this passage could have
been intended for was a puzzle at first.   It
would seem, however, to have been a conduit
or *cloaca* to carry off the water that might
collect in the theatre when heavy rain fell;
for when rain falls in this climate it is almost
tropical in its violence, and ruin would inevitably result if the water had no means of
discharging itself.   This *cloaca*, for such it
really seems to be, is as perfect now as the
day it was finished, and doubtless still on
occasion performs the functions for which it
was originally intended.   Some inscriptions
also remain in the theatre, and a statue of a
draped female figure, which still, although
sadly mutilated, retains some of its original
beauty.   I regret to have to say that our guide,
his antiquarian propensities notwithstanding,
was anxious to mutilate the figure still more,
in order that he might present us with a piece
of the marble to carry away as a memento of
Saguntum, and we had no little difficulty in
restraining his destructive intentions.

The fortifications above the theatre are of vast extent, and the view therefrom is even more striking and interesting than that seen from the cathedral tower of Valencia. The place is now occupied as a military position, and appeared to be in excellent order and repair.

The church of Sta. Maria, in the centre of the town, is well situated. The exterior is very fine, but the interior, in the Græco-Roman style, is heavy and ugly, and by no means what the appearance of the outside would lead one to expect.

There is another very old church in the suburb *del Salvador*, said to be one of the oldest in Spain. There was also a *circus maximus* in ancient times, of which now only a few insignificant remains are visible.

In the market-place we noticed some Roman columns with mutilated capitals supporting the arcades on two of its sides, and doubtless many more such fragments lie hidden away and forgotten elsewhere. In 1795 a magnificent mosaic representing Bacchus riding a tiger and holding the thyrsus, amid wine-growers, bacchantes, &c., was discovered in the neighbourhood, but has since disappeared.

The severity of our antiquarian researches had by this time developed in us a not un natural desire for some light refreshment. But where to find anything was the difficulty, for in unfrequented places in Spain eating and drinking, as most other nations understand these expressions, are not looked upon as matters of very great importance. A little fruit, a crust of bread, and a few go-downs of water fresh from the well are all that are considered necessary. The fine climate and healthy air will supply all deficiencies in the way of diet. The principal *posada* could afford us nothing at all; but with the readily afforded help of some of the inhabitants we discovered a café, where we were able to procure some coffee, served in small cups, and some fresh water. There was no milk or even bread to be had. However we had brought a few provisions with us, wherewith we supplemented the resources of the establishment. It was a clean tidy little place, and the coffee was fairly good. We should have been better pleased, however, if there had been more of the invigorating beverage.

We returned to our headquarters in the

evening tired and hungry, but at the same time delighted at the good day's work we had accomplished.

We left Valencia with regret—*Valencia del Cid*, as it is appropriately called—for how that hero of ballad and chronicle took the city in 1094–5, how he governed it in a dictatorial and absolute manner, how the Moors marched against the city as soon as they became aware of his death, and how they were frightened out of their senses at the stratagem of his wife Ximena, who placed the body of her departed husband upright on his favourite steed Babieca—all this and a good deal more besides, is it not written in the *Chronicle of the Cid*, and well known to English readers through the admirable adaptation of Southey ?

CHAPTER XI.

MADRID—TOLEDO.

FROM Valencia to Madrid, to which latter place we were now obliged to return, is a run, or rather *crawl*, of about sixteen hours. You are in the fertile province of Valencia, and your eye is continually refreshed by the sight of orange trees, palms, and pomegranates until you approach Almansa, where a less fertile and sterner-looking country begins. At Almansa there is a good buffet, where you are allowed time to dine.

The most important place between Valencia and Almansa is Jativa, a Moorish-looking town, built in a beautiful fertile plain at the foot of a range of hills, up the sides of which the battlemented walls of an old fortress have been built in zigzag to the top. The country all about here teems with plenty, and the villages, with their quaint habitations and square brick belfries, capped with many-coloured tiles, sparkling in the sun, give additional effect to the brilliancy of the landscape. The inhabitants, too, have an unmistakably Eastern appearance, thoroughly in keeping with their surroundings.

At Madrid we put up again at the Hôtel de Paris, decidedly a well-appointed inn in every respect, but dear. It is hardly necessary to say that we again devoted a considerable portion of time to the pictures. It was especially interesting to compare the paintings of the Valencian school with those we had recently seen in the headquarters of that school. The Valencian masters are without doubt represented in greater force and variety in their own home than in Madrid; but I do not think there is anything finer in Valencia than the marvellous Last Supper, by Juanes, at Madrid. Ribera, too, is well represented at the royal picture gallery.

We also paid a visit to the *Academia de San Fernando* in the *Calle de Alcalá*, which we had omitted to do the year before. The finest picture here is Murillo's famous St. Elizabeth Healing the Lepers. The beggars to whom the saint is extending her care are such as Murillo himself saw, and are exactly like their successors of the present day, as regards their generally ragged and unsavoury appearance. All this raggedness and unsavouriness, however, only serves to bring into greater relief the dignity and beauty of the saint herself. There are a few other good pictures in this gallery by Ribera, Zurbaran, &c., and a charming *Maja* by Goya, that truly racy and national painter of Spanish life as it existed at the end of the last and the beginning of the present century.

Another visit to Toledo took up one whole day. Toledo is like the Madrid picture gallery; you may keep on going there for ever, and you will always find fresh subjects for admiration and wonder.

On arriving at the railway station we secured the services of an excellent guide, Mariano Portales by name. He proved to be thoroughly acquainted with every nook and corner of the imperial city, and discoursed intelligently on its many and various historical and artistic objects of interest. Another immense recommendation in his favour is that he is *not* acquainted with either French or English, so that you are not called upon to undergo the annoyance of having an imperfectly spoken tongue hurled at your head. Portales holds forth in his own pure Castilian, which is a lesson in itself; for, be it remembered, the Spanish spoken at Toledo is considered the purest, and the peasant speaks as good Castilian as the peer. Our guide, though to all appearance a quiet and unassuming man, was, like a true Spaniard, proud of his descent; and on passing the mansion of an ancient family, with the coat of arms carved, as usual, over the entrance, he produced his card, with his own escutcheon engraved upon it, and informed us that his quarterings were the same as those sculptured on the mansion. It is needless to say that we in no way attempted to throw any doubts on his claim to ancestral honours. Spaniards of all grades of life, even down to the beggars, expect to be treated with consideration, and nothing is more likely to offend them than a want of courtesy. In no country does urbanity carry greater weight; a civil tongue and a gracious manner are more precious than rubies.

We went again over much of the ground we had explored the year before, and visited besides other places where we had not as yet been, among which I will mention, in the first place, the *Casa de Mesa*, the *Taller del Moro*, and the *Mezquita del Cristo de la Luz*, all full of interesting Moorish details, as regards roofing, arching, and wall decorations.

The last-mentioned building is like the mosque of Cordova in miniature, so much does it resemble it in general design as well as in details. From this similarity the learned have not unreasonably inferred that it must belong to the same period of Moorish architecture, and that it was, in all probability, built about the middle of the eleventh century. On Sunday, the 25th May, 1085, Alfonso VI., after making his triumphal entry through the old gate of *Visagra* into the conquered city, stopped before this little building, as it was the first place of worship he met with in his progress. Here he caused the first mass of the new era to be said, the famous Abbot Don Bernard, who was afterwards the first archbishop of the diocese, officiating. On account of this event, and also on account of the anti-

quity of the little mosque, which is said to
have formerly been a church built in Gothic
times, and the miraculous stories told of an
image of Christ in connection therewith, the
archbishop took it under his particular care,
and had it repaired and altered. It is a pity
he had not left it alone, at least as regards
alterations. But happily most of the Moorish
features still remain.

The *Casa de Mesa* stands opposite the
church of San Roman. It is said to have
belonged to the celebrated Don Estaban de
Illan. Little except a fine saloon now remains
to testify to its original magnificence. This
saloon, however, is one of the best specimens
of Saracenic work to be seen anywhere, not
even excepting those found in the principal
cities of Andalusia. The fine and delicate
ornamentation, and the general beauty of the
designs, are especially noteworthy. The
ceiling is *artesonado*, and exquisite. From the
fact that inscriptions are altogether wanting,
and from the general character of the architecture, antiquaries have argued that the
building belongs to the period subsequent to
the conquest of Toledo, during which the

Saracenic influence still continued to prevail.

The dilapidated state of the once sumptuous palace, now called the *Taller del Moro*, forbids my going into raptures over it, but the elegance of its ornamentation must, when in its original freshness and beauty, have rivalled anything to be seen in Seville or Granada. It is called the *Taller del Moro* (the workshop of the Moor), because it was used as a workshop in connection with the cathedral, and as a store for the wood and marble employed in its construction and repair. It seems now to have been turned to still baser purposes, and to have become a place for the manufacture of lucifer-matches. The once beautiful ceilings have become blackened. The delicate tracery, which formerly covered the walls, is almost gone, and devastation has held its sway unchecked. How are the mighty fallen! We recrossed the threshold of the *Taller del Moro*, overcome with sorrow and heaviness of heart at the sight of so much dilapidated splendour.

Our guide also took us to see the court yard, or cloister, of the ancient Dominican convent of *San Pedro Martir*. This once vast and splendid edifice has served in turn as a convent, a barrack, and a provincial museum; but it is now used as an asylum for the poor, and for other charitable purposes. The courtyard—the part of the building that is perhaps the best preserved—is a space of more than 100 feet square, having three tiers of galleries open on all four sides, composed of arches and columns of carved stone, with balustrades of the same material in the two top stories. The most interesting thing, however, in this cloister is an Arab well, with a well-preserved inscription carved round its brim of white marble. The inscription, which has been translated by that learned orientalist, Don Pascual de Gayangos, shows that this brim was constructed in 1045 for another cistern then in the ancient cathedral, at that time the principal mosque of the Moors. The inscription throws no small light on the Moorish history of Toledo, as it helps to fix the succession of the Moorish kings in that city, and gives an idea of the importance of the cathedral at that epoch.

We went into the church of *San Tome* in

order to see the much-vaunted masterpiece of Domenico Theotocopuli (*El Greco*), representing the miraculous burial of the pious Count Orgaz (by whom the church was rebuilt and beautified in the beginning of the fourteenth century), a much overrated and unpleasing work, in my humble estimation, although, without doubt, the figures are powerfully and impressively drawn. Notwithstanding that torches are supposed to be burning, the effect of the whole is ghastly and livid.

Much more interesting to me, in every way, was the charming steeple of the church, a beautiful example of Moorish brickwork, and the only remaining vestige of the original building, which is said to have been a mosque. The date, however, of its erection is uncertain.

The church, with the exception of the steeple, is utterly devoid of interest.

There are several other steeples of this kind in Toledo—that of the church of San Roman is perhaps the most remarkable—and the effect produced by these interesting old towers, as they stand out, with all their quaint details, against the clear blue sky, is truly wonderful.

Before bidding a final farewell to Toledo, I cannot forbear a brief allusion to a mouldering structure near the banks of the Tagus, which is the last object seen by the visitor as he leaves the lordly city on his way back to Madrid. This now desolate ruin was once the sumptuous *Palacio de Galiana*, famous in the legendary history of Toledo.

Here once upon a time dwelt the Princess Galiana, the beautiful daughter of Galafre, Moorish king of Toledo, who, out of affection for his daughter, had built this fairy palace for her, and surrounded it with delicious gardens, abounding in fountains and kiosks, and every charm that Moorish art was capable of producing. This lovely maiden was beloved by Abenzaide, the ferocious Governor of Guadalajara, otherwise known as Bradamante, and described as a giant of formidable proportions. His affection, however, was not returned by the princess, who could not endure him in her presence. She had conceived a tender passion for Charles, son of Pepin, afterwards Charlemagne, who had come to Toledo to assist her father against the King of Cordova, and who had been lodged in this palace by Galafre. It is not wonderful that the great Charles lost his heart to the fair princess; and, as his affection was returned by the young lady, it only remained to get Abenzaide conveniently out of the way in order to accomplish their union. This desirable end was brought about by a duel between Charlemagne and his rival, in which the former carried the day, and the Galiana, " déjà Française jusqu'aux yeux," was only too delighted to accompany her hero back to France, where she complacently embraced Christianity, and was crowned queen amid the acclamations of the people.

A few old walls and broken down towers, where the swallows build their nests, are all that now remains of this once splendid palace; but the legend of Charlemagne and the Princess Galiana will probably still continue to live on, even should every trace of the building be ultimately swept away by the ruthless hand of time.

CHAPTER XII.

WHILE in Madrid I made two more fruitless attempts to see the armoury. The first time the custodian was away, either at his dinner or his *siesta*; the next time I found an announcement hung up on the door to the effect that there was to be no admittance while certain works were in progress. There is nothing now left for me but to try and persuade myself, if I can, that there is little really worth seeing in the collection, in the same manner as the fox in the fable endeavoured to depreciate the tempting-looking grapes which hung high up out of his reach.

" Fit-il pas mieux que de se plaindre ? "

We stopped a couple of days at San Sebastian on our way back to Paris. We found little there to gratify our antiquity-hunting propensities, as our countrymen good-

naturedly destroyed nearly the whole of the
old town in 1813. The new town which has
arisen since then is much too clean, bright,
and prosperous to be artistically interesting,
and the churches are hardly worth entering.
But to make up for these lamentable deficiencies, the view from the summit of the Monte
Orgullo is magnificent, and the peasantry,
especially as seen in the market-place in the
morning, very interesting. The Basque
damsels are especially fair to look upon. The
sea beach, too, is beautiful, and tolerably lively
in the afternoon, when the bathers disport
themselves in the water. In the evening the
band plays on the principal promenade, and
crowds of people assemble and walk up and
down; the fashionable people, or those who
consider themselves so, on one side, and the
peasants on the other. The music is very
good, and groups of country people may be
seen dancing prettily to it, whenever the
rhythm will allow them to do so. If they
cannot have a waltz or a galop, a march will
do, but they are rather put out by the slow
movement of a symphony, or the introduction
to an overture.

Our last expedition on Spanish soil was to Fontarabia, or Fuenterrabia, as it is called by the natives. We started by the early train from San Sebastian, and, after a journey of about three-quarters of an hour through the smiling country that lies between that town and the frontier, we alighted at Irun, where we purposed to charter a vehicle to transport us to Fontarabia, and to take us to Hendaye on the French side, but at no great distance, where we intended picking up the express for Bayonne, instead of coming back to Irun again. We soon made a bargain with the smart young driver of a small omnibus, and reached our destination in about half an hour.

Our English guide-books give but scanty information with regard to Fontarabia, and only allude to it as if it were worthy of a mere passing glance. This seems to me to be a very serious omission. It is true that it is possible to explore the whole place in a very short space of time, but nevertheless, diminutive as it unquestionably is, it is a perfect little gem in its way, at all events to those who have a fashion of looking at things through artistic or antiquarian spectacles.

To begin with, the little town possesses a marked Spanish character, which is more than can be said of San Sebastian. Its old houses, blackened with age, are adorned with marvellously carved wooden balconies, grated windows, and overhanging roofs, which nearly meet at the top. Nothing more fascinating can be imagined than the principal street leading up to the church from the ruined gate at the entrance to the town.

The foundation of the Castillo is attributed to Sancho Abarca, king of Navarre, who reigned about 907. It was extended and fortified by *Sancho el Fuerte.* This citadel is composed of two distinct parts, the façade on the *plaza,* which dates from the latter part of the sixteenth century, and some constructions behind it of a much earlier date, which overlook the Bidassoa. These latter are fast falling to ruins; indeed the aspect of the whole building is sombre and melancholy in the extreme. Inside the principal entrance a board is hung up in a conspicuous place, on which is painted an announcement in very indifferent *English* that this interesting relic of the past is for sale. There does not seem to be any probability that the said board will soon be called upon to abrogate its functions. An Englishman at all events would be much more likely to invest his money in a factory in good working order than in an old half-ruined castle.

There are several other *palacios* in this curious old town. They are now mostly in a ruinous state, but their existence proves the former importance of the place. Their façades, adorned with huge escutcheons, are good examples of the solid heavy grandeur which is a distinctive feature of the Spanish renaissance. In these mansions the grandees of former days used to pass the summer season, as those of the present day do in more ornate, though perhaps less solidly constructed, villas in San Sebastian.

The fortifications surrounding the town have been much battered in the numerous wars which have at various times raged over this ill-fated territory. Louis XI., Francis I., Richelieu, and Napoleon have each in their turn assaulted its walls, not to mention the Carlists in 1837. It would not appear, however, that

> . . . "Charlemain with all his peerage fell
> By Fontarabbia,"

as Milton would have us believe, for "Charle-
main" did not fall on any field of battle, but
died in his bed, at Aix-la-Chapelle, on the
28th January, 814, and the direful calamity
referred to, which became so fertile a theme
of song and romance, took place not here,
but at Roncesvalles, in the Pyrenees, some
forty miles away.

Our explorations over, we were met by our
Jehu at the gate where we came in—he having
in the meantime changed his omnibus for a
neat, light-rolling little phaeton. On our
way to Hendaye, through the pleasant valley
of the Bidassoa, we passed close to the famous
"Ile des Faisans," where so many notable
negotiations, conferences, and exchanges have
taken place. This historic island was at one
time in danger of being gradually washed
away by the waters of the river. Under
Napoleon III., however, a quay was erected,
at the expense of Spain and France, with a
view to arresting further destruction, and a
monument was also put up in the centre of
the island. We arrived at Hendaye in time
for a good breakfast at the well-furnished
buffet there.

Thus ended our tour in Spain No. 2, and Fontarabia, with its charming surroundings and interesting historical associations, was a worthy *bonne bouche* to wind up with. For character and picturesqueness, indeed, it cannot be surpassed in its own peculiar way.

We should like to have visited many other towns in Spain, but they must keep for another time. We are painfully conscious of the necessity of atoning for not a few sins of *omission* as well as *commission* during our wanderings. But we have in any case laid in a stock of wholesome and agreeable food for reflection, which will last us for many a long day to come.

CHAPTER XIII.

CONCLUSION.

I WILL now, in conclusion, sum up the result of our impressions of Spain gained during our sojournings in that country.

There is not the least difficulty about travelling anywhere now. The only objection is that the journeys are extremely long, and the trains, as a rule, remarkably slow. The best trains almost invariably run at night, which is a great objection to those who are unable to stand night travelling on railways. We found the officials invariably very civil; even the dreaded custom-house officers were far less formidable than we had been led to expect, and they passed our unostentatious luggage at Irun and Portbou after a merely nominal rummage.

We did not find the hotels, as a rule, so good and comfortable as French hotels, nor did we expect to do so; but they are certainly

better and more reasonable than English
hotels of a similar class. The food is fairly
good and sufficiently varied; but, unfortunately, much of it is spoiled by the very
inferior, not to say decidedly nasty oil used
in the cooking of it. This is chiefly apparent
in dishes of vegetables, such as artichokes,
&c., and in salads. We found these dishes
quite uneatable. It is marvellous that, in a
country where olives abound, the natives
should not yet have learned the art of refining
the oil made from them. The cookery in
vogue at all the hotels in the principal towns
is an imitation of the French system, and
would, but for the inferiority of the oil, leave
little, if anything, to be desired. The meals
are distributed much in the same manner as
in France. You have chocolate or coffee in
the morning, breakfast (at the *table d'hôte* or
à la carte) at eleven, and dinner at six. I
thought the chocolate excellent, at all events,
for a change. With it is usually served a
glass of water and *azucarillos*, compositions
made of sugar, which melt away quickly in
the water, which then has a pleasant refreshing taste, something like lemonade.

The famous Spanish national dish, the *puchero*, or *olla podrida*, occasionally made its appearance at dinner. It is composed of scraps of meat, bacon, sausages, and vegetables mixed up with rice. It is by no means a despicable mess for a hungry traveller. The favourite dish in Valencia is *arroz a la Valenciana* (riz à la mode de Valence); I think it excellent. Some people, however, might be led to form an unfavourable opinion of this dish on account of the garnish of *fried snails* which usually accompanies it. Such persons would probably prefer that the snails, if served at all, should appear separately. But to the mode of serving the rice itself no objection can possibly be raised, whatever may be thought of the garnish.

Butter is rarely met with. When it does appear it is generally uneatable, and tastes like indifferent cooking butter, or second-rate Dorset. But on the other hand, the bread, except a peculiar close kind which we did not like, is excellent, as also the cheese. There is also plenty of choice confectionery, and an abundance of fruit, especially grapes.

An improvement might, I think, be effected in the ordinary wine put on the tables at breakfast and dinner. It is not usually a very palatable beverage.

We always found our beds clean and well aired, and on no occasion were we molested by any noisome insects, except the inevitable mosquito in the South. The beds are not provided with pillows, but only with bolsters, of which there are two, one placed on the top of the other. The stuffing of these parts of the bed rniture is not always all that could be desired. They are not so much, however, hard as *lumpy*, a state of things not very conducive to slumber. But trifles like these are soon overcome.

The cost of living in the best hotels is usually from 40 to 50 reals a day, and it is well to ask beforehand what is included and what is left out of the charge, as you will thus be saved the annoyance of a discussion when the bill is. produced. The servants expect a trifle in addition to the usual charge for service in the bill, but they are not grasping.

In all the principal towns there are good

cafés, where excellent coffee is to be had. If
you want a *café noir*, you ask for *café solo :*
if with milk you say *café con leche*, and you
only pay twopence-halfpenny, except in
Madrid, where · the price of everything is
higher than in the provinces.

The brigands have not yet been quite
exterminated in Spain, but they have been
considerably *thinned* by that efficient and
well-organised corps, the *Guardia Civil*, or
gendarmes. While we were in the country
a band of these malefactors, who had formed
a project for stopping the Andalusian train,
was arrested in a forest near Toledo by the
gendarmerie. Four or five of the bandits,
including the chief of the gang, a notorious
criminal, and the terror of the villages of La
Mancha, were killed. The neighbourhood
had suffered severely from the depredations
of these robbers. The gendarmes are well
armed, and patrol generally two together.
They are to be seen everywhere, and are a
real terror to evildoers. We met them at
intervals along the road we traversed in the
diligence. But notwithstanding all their
efforts a few brigands still manage to live,

if not to thrive, in wild and inaccessible places in the mountains.

The following details of the capture and escape of Mr. John Lester, of Lowestoft, from Spanish brigands near San Sebastian, were published a short while back, and are worth reproducing here if only as a warning to others.

Mr. Lester writes:—" I had walked about sixty miles through some of the grandest scenery in the North of Spain, and wishing to cross the French frontier that night, was pushing on rather late, when about nine o'clock, and in a lonely part of the road, bordered with woods, midway between San Sebastian and Irun, I was accosted by a Spaniard, who asked a few simple questions, walking along by my side at the time. Some others had been either following or had stepped out from amongst the trees. I was suddenly felled to the ground from behind, and on recovering consciousness some hours afterwards found myself in a dilapidated house or hovel, tied by the leg to a fastening in a corner of the smaller of its two divisions, stripped of all but my trousers and

M

shirt, and with a bundle of straw for my bed. I will not attempt to describe my feelings on finding myself in such a position alone with, and at the mercy of, a gang of bloodthirsty robbers, perhaps infuriated at not gaining as much as they expected. Day succeeded day, without anything of note being said. I was supplied with bread and water, and I found the gang to consist of five men, three of whom were but indifferently armed. My capture had been effected on the night of Friday, July 8th. On what I found afterwards to have been the night of Friday, July 15th, having lost count of the days during my monotonous incarceration, thinking I had had sufficient of that place, and, moreover, being tormented with feelings of hunger, not having had anything given me since the previous evening, and having an idea that their neglect was a preliminary to my death in some shape or other, I resolved to strive for liberty. Having worked out a stone which I found rather loose in the wall near me, and having taken advantage of the darkness of my corner, I gnawed asunder the cord that bound me. I made to the door, which opened into the other apartment, and there being but one guard left over me—the others being off on some expedition—I watched for an opportunity. Presently it was afforded me. As the fellow sat with his back towards me, resting his head upon his hands, I stole forward, holding my stone in readiness, and with one blow laid him on the floor. Then, snatching up a knife from the table, I ran out, and, after wandering amongst the mountains most of the night, found myself at daybreak on the highway, with my feet cut with the stones and my strength gone. I fainted. On coming round I attempted in vain to rise, when two men coming along with a bullock-cart, I asked for help. All they did was to prod me with their goads and march on. The labourers now turning to their work in the fields, and seeing my attempt to regain my feet, several of them pelted me with clods. I had little strength left, but at last I managed to get on my feet, and having rested awhile to regain my strength, I staggered along to the town, and waited upon the vice-consul, who kindly provided me with food and clothes, after which I accompanied him before the governor of the province to make my statement. Being then weak and ill, I found it necessary to enter the hospital for a few days, and am now gaining strength among the mountains of Biscay. The Spanish Government have the matter under consideration ; but, as they do not undertake to indemnify persons from any injury perpetrated by their subjects, I am told on good authority that I shall be lucky if they but allow me for what I have lost."

It is impossible to help feeling for Mr. Lester in his misfortunes, but one is tempted nevertheless to ask, like Géronte, " Que diable allait-il faire dans cette galère ? " Travelling in Spain is safe on the whole, so it is in England, but there are still some parts of London where it is better not to venture without the protection of a policeman.

The zeal of the Spanish police, however, sometimes outruns their discretion, as has been recently shown in the case of the Pastor Fliedner, and in other cases accounts of which have been published. A friend of mine, who has been much in Spain, was acquainted with the captain of a company of these Guardias. My friend being anxious to have some shooting at large game, asked his friend, the captain, if he would put him in the way of obtaining what he wanted. The captain said he should be most happy to assist him in every way in his power, and invited him to his station, telling him he thought he would certainly be able to give him some sport, as there were still, he believed, *a few brigands left* in the mountains near. As my friend's definition of "large game" did not exactly include *brigands*, the kind offer of the captain was politely declined. On the whole, however, it must be admitted that the *Guardia Civil* is a highly efficient corps, and a credit to Spain.

The water-drinking propensities of the Spaniards are well known. Water-carriers abound in the streets, at the railway stations, at bull-fights, and all places of public resort. When the train stops at stations, one of the first sounds heard is, "*Agua! agua! quien quiere agua?*" or sometimes it is "*Agua y agua ardiente!*" i.e. a kind of spirit and water. The water is usually excellent, and is generally sold with the *azucarillos* before mentioned.

But whence it is procured is not always apparent. The Moors performed wonders in the way of irrigation, and the beneficial effects of some of their work have not yet been obliterated. Many of the wells made by them still exist, and the water drawn from those wells is highly prized on account of its sweetness and purity, for it is well known that they spared no pains in penetrating to the best springs and fountains. The *Plaza de los Algibes* (the place or square of the cisterns), within the fortress of the Alhambra, is undermined by reservoirs, which receive the waters of the Darro, and have been in existence since the time of the Moors. In the corner of this square is a famous draw-well cut through the rock to an immense depth, which is still, as it has been for ages past, the rendezvous of the water-carriers and gossips of the neighbourhood.

It is in the province of Valencia that the beneficial effects of the system of irrigation instituted by the Arabs are most apparent. The soil is luxuriously productive, and the whole province teems with fertility and verdure. But so important is irrigation to the productiveness of the ground, that a tribunal called *El Tribunal de las Aguas* (the tribunal of the waters), has been erected for the purpose of determining *las cuestiones de riego* (irrigation questions). Those who have been guilty of unduly abstracting the water belonging to their neighbours, or of hoarding it up unfairly for their own exclusive use and profit, are here called upon to give an account of their misdoings. This singular court, which has been in existence since the year 920, is still kept up in all its patriarchal and oriental simplicity. The judges, called *Sindicos*, are simple peasants elected by their fellows. The sittings take place on a comfortable sofa under the porch of the Cathedral of Valencia every Thursday at 12 o'clock. No advocates are employed to represent the parties interested, nor are any other officers required; but a rough and ready sort of justice is meted out, which appears to answer its purpose, and to satisfy those concerned.

I must not forget to mention another relic of bygone times, which still lingers in old Spanish towns. I refer to the watchmen. Their chief business seems to be to patrol the streets at night, and call the hour, adding their report as to the state of the weather for the information of all whom it may concern. Hence their name *Serenos*, for they usually wind up with the announcement that the weather is *sereno*, i. e. fine. They must be much like what the old watchmen were in English towns in former days. I do not know whether it is part of their duty " to comprehend all vagrom men," but I should be inclined to imagine that such functions would be better discharged by the *Guardia Civil.* They wear a long cloak, and carry a lantern and a staff. When in Cordova I was so fortunate as to see the Dogberry of the place giving his " charge" to his " good men and true" before dismissing them to their rounds. It would have been almost worth while going all that way to see that sight alone.

Another charm about Spain is that it is not yet overrun in the same manner as other parts of the continent. It has so far remained comparatively unpolluted by the presence of that singular product of modern civilisation, the unmitigated British tourist—I mean the curious individual who insists upon carrying with him, wherever he goes, all his insular prejudices and eccentricities, as snails do their houses, who makes no attempt to conform to the usages, or learn the language of the people among whom he travels, and who must have his bacon and eggs, his tea and toast, his *lunch* and his lawn-tennis, whether such things are indigenous to the soil or not. We were so fortunate as to meet with travelling companions of a decidedly higher order than those above referred to. We fell in with English, French, Germans, Portuguese, and a solitary Dutchman, and we found them for the most part agreeable and intelligent people.

But with improving accommodation, and increased facilities for travelling, it must be expected that Spain will be sought after as other European countries have been. With the gain, however, there is sure to be some loss. But in any case I hope to go back there again as soon as circumstances will allow me to do so.

As regards the language, I derived much assistance from a book of dialogues with the

title, 'L'Espagnol tel qu'on le parle, ou re-
cueil de conversations espagnoles et françaises,
avec la prononciation figurée par des sons
français, à l'usage des Français qui vont en
Espagne, par José M. Lopes.' It has been
observed with as much wit as truth that
books of this sort "are chiefly remarkable for
never in any instance containing anything
that any one would have occasion to say to
any one else under any circumstances whatever." But 'L'Espagnol tel qu'on le parle' is
an exception to this somewhat sweeping
verdict, and does not belie its title. I found
it a decidedly useful collection of phrases.
For the rest, in addition to the help to be
obtained from grammars and dictionaries, the
best way to make progress is to read as much
as possible, and, above all things, to keep
one's ears wide open, listen keenly to what
the people met with in the country say,
adopting the phrases *used by them* as part of
one's own mental system—such phrases to be
carefully stored up in the memory, and
brought out again as occasion may require.
Those who adopt the opposite plan, viz. of
manufacturing phrases of their own, solely

with the aid of grammar and dictionary, will, in all probability, produce something which, whatever it may be, will not be Spanish, and they will run the chance of failing altogether to convey their meaning to the natives.

If the above remarks are correct, they will of course apply with equal force to the acquisition of any foreign language whatever.

The literature of Spain is a rich and varied one, as English and American readers familiar with Mr. Ticknor's valuable 'History of Spanish Literature,' hardly require to be reminded; and fortunately the cream of it is now placed within reach of the slenderest purses through the medium of the 'Biblioteca Universal,' or 'Coleccion de los mejores Autores Antiguos y Modernos, Nacionales y Extranjeros,' now in course of publication. These volumes are carefully edited, and neatly printed on good paper, and cost only two reals (fivepence) each. A list of those that had appeared up to the time of our last leaving the country is subjoined.

Romancero del Cid ..	1	F. L. de Leon y San
La Celestina	2 & 3	Juan de la Cruz .. 5
La Edad Media	4	Poesias alemanas .. 6

Proudhon	7	Lope, Nieto de Molina	
Romancero Morisco	8 & 10	y Castro	38
Cervántes	9	Castillejo	39
Herculano	11	Schiller	40
Espronceda	12	Eusebio Blasco	41
Goethe	13	Victor Hugo	42 & 44
Larra	14 & 15	Poesías mejicanas	45
Romancero Caballeresco	16	Melo	46, 47 & 49
Tesoro de la poesía		Campoamor	48
Castellana 17, 18, 20, 22 & 30		Mesonero Romanos	51 & 52
El Diablo Mundo	19	Bossuet	53
Dante, Tasso y Pe-		Mirabeau	54
trarca	21	Eurípides	55
Tirso de Molina	23	Voltaire	56
Calderon de la Barca	24	Víctor Balaguer	57
Fray Lope de Vega	25	Escritoras españolas	58
Zorrilla	26	Tarass Boulba	59
Quevedo	27, 28 & 32	Poetas americanos	60
Soulié	43 & 50	Jovellanos	61
Balzac	29	Poetas contemporáneos	62 & 64
Santa Teresa	31	Lord Byron—Poemas	63
Alarcon	33	Ventura Ruiz Aguilera	65
La casada perfecta	34	Marco Polo	66
Ramon de la Cruz	35	Cristóbal Colon	67
Quevedo—Poesías	36	D. Cárlos	68 & 69
Moratin	37	El Universo en la ciencia	70

It is needless to say that we filled our pockets with a goodly selection of them before we came away.

The idea of the *coleccion* would seem to have been taken from the " Bibliothéque Nationale" in France. The volumes in the latter collection only cost *twopence-halfpenny* each, but the Spanish volumes are rather better "got up." Both collections contain translations of eminent foreign authors, as well as native original works, and the advantages they give the humble student are incalculable

In connection with the recent progress of literature in Spain, the following paper by Señor J. F. Riaño, which appeared in the *Athenæum* for the 31st December, 1881, will be read with interest.

"The tendency to general improvement which I noticed last year, as indicative of a decided progress in everything connected with science and letters, has now become patent. Peace, a Liberal Government, reforms in the administration which all parties, however extreme, seem willing to accept and acknowledge, an improved system of education extended to every class of society, cannot fail to secure for Spain that position among European nations to which her former history, geographical situation, fertile soil, and mineral resources entitle her.

"The improvement is visible in all branches of literature. During the present year several important works have been published, and the various 'philobiblon' and 'text printing societies,' in the provinces as well as in the capital, have displayed much activity, publishing for the first time or reprinting many important works, which either lurked still inedited in the obscure corners of a public library, or were so scarce and valuable as to call for their immediate reprint. Thus the Madrid 'Bibliófilos,' after reprinting (with a learned, if short, introduction by the Marquis de la Fuente del Valle) Padilla's 'Romancero,' have now published for the first time the 'Relacion de la Jornada de Pedro de Ursúa á Omagua y al Dorado,' by an anonymous writer, which, being the narrative of the singularly stirring events through which that governor met his death, as well as a faithful picture of the atrocities committed in those parts by Pedro de Aguirre, cannot fail to engross the attention of the historical student in those remote provinces of South America. This, I hear, is soon to be followed—perhaps whilst I am tracing these lines the printing is already finished—by the 'Cancionero General de Hernando del Castillo,' first printed at Valencia in 1511, folio, and perhaps ten or twelve more times during the sixteenth century—a work which, notwithstanding it has passed through numerous editions, required more than any other of its kind a new one, both critical and corrected, showing the many discrepancies, additions, and suppressions of the former ones, and above all, giving us notices of the courtly poets and popular rhymesters who contributed to Castillo's collection. I sincerely hope that Señor Balenchana, to whom the 'Bibliófilos' of this capital have entrusted the arduous task of editing the work, may fulfil it to the satisfaction of students of Spanish literature.

"Of the 'Documentos Inéditos para la Historia de España' two more volumes, the seventy-sixth and seventy-seventh, have appeared. 'Guerras del Perú' is the title of the first, by that well-known historian of South America, Pedro Cieza de Leon. The second is a history, hitherto inedited, of the reign of Philip IV., intended as a continuation of that of his father, Philip III., formerly attributed to Barnabé de Vibanco, but which latter researches lead us to suppose was the work of his kinsman, Novoa.

" The Royal Geographical Society, inaugurated by King Alfonso three years ago, have now completed the tenth volume of their transactions, and one-half of the eleventh. These transactions come out in monthly numbers. 'Expedicion Española á Abisinia'; 'Las Islas Hauaii,' by Beltran y Rózpide; 'El Istmo de Tehuantepec,' by Arrangoiz; 'La Geografia de España del Edrisi,' by Eduardo Saavedra; 'Canales Interoceánicos,' by Justo Zaragoza; and 'Dictámen acerca del Viaje proyectado por La Esploradora, asociacion Euskara para la exploracion del Africa,' are among the interesting papers read by members of the society, and published in the above-mentioned volumes. Nor are these the only publications of the kind. I may further mention: 'Notas y Apuntes de un Viaje por el Pirenéo,' by Antonio Maria Fabié; 'Viaje al Interior de Persia,' by Ribadeneyra; 'Disquisiciones Nauticas,' by Fernandez Duro; 'Los Judios en España.' by Fray Tinéo Heredia; 'España en Berberia,' by Marcos Jimenez de la Espada; and last, not least, 'La Rusia Contemporánea: Bocetos Historicos,' by that distinguished orator, statesman, and writer, Don Emilio Castelar; all publica-

and Verdaguer at Barcelona, Velarde at Seville, and a host of other poets less known or now making their first excursions to Parnassus, show that the taste for rhyming is not altogether extinct in Spain.

"Of Campoamor's nice little volume of poetry entitled 'Los Buenos y los Sabios,' of Echegaray's 'Gran Galeoto,' and Zorilla's 'Recuerdos del Tiempo Viejo,' I can only say that they must be mentioned with praise; the authors are veterans, and know well how to please the public. The same may be said of novelists like Fernandez y Gonzalez, Valera, Alarcon, Blasco, Pereda, and many more; they have long amused the public with their lively fictions. The first named, who is called by Spaniards the Walter Scott of Spain, has certainly surpassed that celebrated novelist in the number of his works if he has not approached him in point of talent, historical learning, and knowledge of character and manners in past ages. Within the present year I have seen and read two new novels by him, 'La Sobrina del Cura' and 'La Leyenda de Madrid.' 'Medina Zahara,' an historical legend by Alcalde, is well deserving of notice,

as well as his 'Canto Epico de Lepanto,'
perhaps the sole attempt in epic poetry made
this year in Spain.   A fresh edition of ' Ayer,
Hoy y Mañana,' by Antonio Flores, a popular
writer and poet, now dead, and the collected
works of the late Adelardo Lopez de Ayala
in two volumes, besides 'Nuevos Cantos,' by
Narcisso Campillo, 'El Primer Loco,' by Doña
Rosalia Castro de Murguia, and 'Heliodora,'
an operetta (*zarzuela*) by the son of the
much-regretted Hartzenbusch, are perhaps
the only productions in light literature worth
mentioning in this article.

"The 'Cervantistas,' as they style themselves, have been comparatively idle of late.
There have been no more essays from the
pens of Assensio, Mainez, and Sbarbi; no
more pamphlets by Castro, Benjumea, and
others; in fact it would seem as if we were
to be relieved for a time of the ponderous,
somewhat conjectural, and at times extravagant erudition with which the students
of Spanish literature in general, and the
lovers of Cervantes in particular, have been
troubled for the last five years.   Indeed, the
affections and sympathies of Spaniards would

appear to have been suddenly transferred to another national idol, the great Don Pedro Calderon de la Barca, whose second centenary was celebrated last May with much pomp and splendour. Innumerable compositions in prose or verse poured in upon this "muy heróica villa de Madrid" from all parts of the ancient Spanish monarchy, from America and the Philippine Islands, as well as from Portugal and Germany; and the festival has brought forth a selection of Calderon's dramatic works in four volumes, by Menendez Pelayo; an ' Album Calderoniano,' by Spanish and Portuguese poets; 'Homenage á Calderon,' anonymous; and several more works. Such almost phenomenal enthusiasm must be explained by the fact that the academies, the central university, and other literary or scientific corporations had previously offered substantial prizes for the best essay or poem in praise of the great dramatist. For instance, the Royal Academy of History offered a prize for the best critical essay on the 'Magico Prodigioso' of Calderon, and more particularly on the relative merits of that drama as compared with those of the

' Faust ' of Goethe. Sanchez Moguel, a young
and promising author, obtained the prize,
proving in an erudite essay that the legend
of Ciprian, ' the Magician,' has nothing in
common with that of Dr. Faust.   In a like
manner Don Adolfo de Castro obtained from
another academy, that of Moral and Political
Sciences, a prize for his essay on the senti-
ments, the manners and customs of Spaniards
in the seventeenth century as described in
Calderon's dramas.   Several editions, moreover, of single and detached plays of our
great dramatist, such as ' La Vida es Sueño,'
and others, appeared at Zamora, Salamanca,
and other provincial towns, thus showing
that, for the time being at least, the enthusiasm has not been limited to the capital,
but has reached all corners of the Spanish
monarchy.

" Scarcely three months had elapsed since
Calderon's second centenary, with its civic
processions and gorgeous pageants, when, in
September last, the congress of American
scholars and writers (Congreso de los Ameri-
canistas) met.   That it was well attended by
delegates from all quarters of the globe,

and especially from France, Belgium, and
Germany, as well as from remote parts of
America where the Spanish language is still
in use; that its meetings began on the 25th
of September by an appropriate inaugural
address from King Alfonso himself; and
that in the intervals of its sessions a most
interesting museum, consisting exclusively of
relics of past civilisations in North and South
America, was inspected by the members, also
invited to the Escurial and to Toledo—we
need not stop to say, as the 'Acta' of the
congress, together with the king's inaugural
speech on the occasion, have been published,
conjointly with a detailed and classified
catalogue of all the objects composing the
so-called 'Exposicion Americanista.' But
I cannot pass over in silence the splendid
volume entitled " Relaciones Geográficas de
Indias,' tomo i., which the Ministerio de
Fomento has just now published for distribu-
tion among the members of the congress.
The editor is that same Marcos Jimenez de
la Espada, the indefatigable writer on the
geography and history of South America,
whose name is frequently found in the pages

of the *Athenæum.* The 'Relaciones' are all
original, and taken from the Archivo de
Indias in Seville, a vast repository of papers
and documents relating to America and Asia
in general and to the West Indies in particular. They form part of a collection prepared in Philip II.'s time with a view to a
statistical and political survey of the vast
Spanish monarchy in the sixteenth century.

"In the department of history I may record
here a few works, such as 'Las Ordenes
Religiosas,' by Antequera; 'Historia Critico-
Filosofica de la Monarquia Asturiana,' by
Menendez Valdés; 'Galeria de Jesuitas
Illustres,' by Father Fidel Fita of the Society
of Jesus; 'Historia de los Heterodoxos Es-
pañoles,' vol. ii., by Marcelino Menendez
Pelayo; 'Doña Ana de Silva y Mendoza'
(the princess of Eboli?) by Julian Saenz de
Tejada; 'Bosquejo Biográfico de Don Beltran
de la Cueva,' by Rodriguez Villa; and
'Boceto Historico: Cánovas, su Pasado, su
Presente y su Porvenir,' by Saurin; most of
which, if not all, have been well received by
he reading public.

"So much for the literary movement in the

capital; that in the provinces, if not so vigorous and active, is showing signs of improvement. In former times, when Spain was an aggregate of various kingdoms, and the court was shifting from one city to another, the press in the provinces was flourishing. Burgos, Toledo, Valladolid, and Medina del Campo in Castile; Seville and Granada in Andalusia; Saragossa, Barcelona, and Valencia in Aragon; and Lisbon during the period of Spanish domination from 1580 to 1640, may be said to have produced the oldest and finest specimens of printing. When, however, Philip III., after three years passed at Valladolid, was persuaded by his favourite Lerma to return to Madrid, and declare it the capital of the Spanish monarchy, a great part of the vitality of the provincial towns was absorbed by the 'heróica villa.' Yet in order to prove to my readers that a provincial and almost federative spirit still lives in the hearts of the people, I will only mention as examples the 'Cancionero Basco,' by Monterola; 'La Danza, Poesia Bable,' by Cuesta; 'Las Libertades de Aragon,' by Danvila; the 'Discurso de la Comunidad de

Sevilla,' by Benitez de Lugo; 'La Inundacion de Levante,' by Bermejo; and 'Estudi de Toponomástica Catalana,' by Sanpere y Miguel, a work of great research—all of which demonstrate that Galicians as well as Asturians, the Basques and the Catalans, are doing all they can to preserve their languages or dialects, and save their separate histories from oblivion. Laudable efforts of this sort are daily being made at Barcelona, where the cultivation of science and literature has lately made such progress as to render this great commercial city in many respects almost a rival to Madrid itself. I have neither time nor space to follow out here the rapid advance which Barcelona, Tarragona, Lérida, Gerona, and other towns of Catalonia, and generally of the "Coronilla de Aragon," so called, are making. Suffice it to say that Barcelona possesses no less than twenty illustrated journals, including six monthly magazines and reviews, and that three months ago one of its most enterprising publishers (C. Verdaguer) brought forth a biographical notice of Fortuny, illustrated with photo-engravings by Goupil reproducing, on a smaller scale and with perfect success, the best works of that celebrated artist, a native of Barcelona. The volume, which is to form part of a larger work, entitled "Biblioteca de Artes y Letras," is handsomely printed and beautifully got up, though the transfer to zinc plates of Goupil's photographs might have been better executed. The binding is both elegant and classical, and the letterpress has been written by José Yxart."

For a concise and trustworthy account of Spanish art I would refer to the same accomplished writer's 'Essay on Spanish Art' prefixed to the Catalogue of Spanish Works of Art recently exhibited in the Loan Collection at the Kensington Museum.

I would also mention the Rev. Wentworth Webster's recently published book on Spain, which contains much useful information on these and other topics in connection with that wonderfully interesting country.

SUMMARY OF THE PRINCIPAL EVENTS IN
SPANISH HISTORY.

For the convenience of those of my readers who may desire to possess some slight information on the neglected subject of the history of Spain, I subjoin the following short summary of the principal events in the annals of that country.

The earlier history of Spain, like that of most other countries, is enveloped in obscurity. The Iberians are the first inhabitants referred to by historians, and of these the Basques in the north are supposed to be the descendants. The Celts subsequently penetrated into the Peninsula, and, becoming at length more or less mingled with the Iberians, the two races are spoken of by the common name of Celtiberians.

The Phœnicians, attracted by the fertility and mineral wealth of the country, established colonies at a very early period at several places on the sea coast. The Carthaginians succeeded them, having been attracted in like manner by the gold and silver mines with which the country abounded. They were the first to obtain firm footing in it; but they, in their turn, were expelled by the Romans, who remained in possession during the existence of their empire in the west.

Under the Government of Rome the Latin language became general, and both learning and commerce were extensively cultivated. Many celebrated Roman authors were natives of this country, among whom may be mentioned the poets Lucan and Martial, and the philosopher Seneca. Spain can also boast of having given birth to two of the very few good Roman emperors, viz. Trajan and Hadrian.

Upon the overthrow of the Roman empire, Spain was overrun by an irruption of northern barbarians, the Suevi, the Vandals, and the Alani. The dominion of the Goths, which followed, lasted for a period of nearly three centuries, from 415 to 711; when the Saracens, or Moors, invaded the country, defeated Roderick, the last of the Gothic kings, in the battle of the Guadalete, near Xeres; and, in about eight months, succeeded in making themselves masters of almost the whole country.

A remnant, however, of the old inhabitants escaped, and took refuge in the mountains of the Asturias. They elected the gallant Don Pelayo, a Gothic prince, and cousin of Roderick, as their king, who, with his scanty following, frequently sallied forth from his headquarters in the cavern of Covadonga, and caused much havoc among the Moors. Thus began the contest between Moors and Christians in Spain, which lasted for nearly eight centuries, during which period as many as three thousand seven hundred battles are said to have been fought.

In the meantime the Christians had succeeded in establishing several small kingdoms, such as those of Navarre, Leon, Castile, and Aragon; but their petty sovereigns were constantly at war with each other. Such was also the case among the princes of the Moorish dominions; indeed it was no uncommon policy for the Christian princes to form alliances with the Moors against each other. Disunion thus prevailed in about equal measure on both sides, and hence the ultimate subjugation of the country by the Christians was retarded for many years.

Eventually, by the marriage of Ferdinand, king of

Aragon, with Isabella, Queen of Castile, the monarchies of Aragon and Castile became united. In this reign Granada, the last city retained by the Moors in Spain, was taken in 1492, and the Moorish dominion in the country fell for ever. In the same year the new world was discovered by Christopher or Christobal Columbus, an event which greatly augmented the glory and greatness of Spain. The greatest calamity in this eventful reign was the institution of the odious Inquisition at the instigation of Torquemada. This fearful tribunal executed its audacious sentences with merciless and unsparing cruelty, and was the means of impressing on the mind of the people a state of torpor and inactivity, whereby lasting injury was inflicted on the country. Isabella died in 1504, and Ferdinand in 1516.

Under the sway of Ferdinand's grandson, Charles V., Spain rose to her greatest height of splendour, but the liberties of the people received many crushing blows. Charles resigned his extensive hereditary dominions to his son Philip II., and retired to the monastery of Yuste, near Placentia in Estremadura, where he died in 1558, aged 58.

The character of Philip II. is sufficiently well known, and his attempted invasion of England by means of his "Invincible" Armada need not be enlarged upon. His tyranny and cruel bigotry in the Low Countries occasioned the loss of the United Provinces, which became independent states. This gloomy and inhuman monarch died in 1598.

A succession of weak superstitious princes followed, till at last the Austrian line failed in the person of Charles II., who died without issue in 1700. A war then arose for the succession to the Spanish dominions, which was at last determined in favour of Philip, Duke of

Anjou, grandson of Louis XIV. of France, by the treaty of Utrecht, 1713.

Of the princes who succeeded, Charles III. (1759-1788) showed the most ability, or perhaps we should rather say, the least incapacity. In 1808 his feeble successor, Charles IV., was induced to abdicate in favour of his son, Ferdinand VII., who, in his turn, was forced to relinquish his throne by Napoleon, who decoyed him to Bayonne, and endeavoured to crown his own brother Joseph King of Spain. The events which followed are, or ought to be, familiar to all. The inhabitants rose as one man in defence of their rights, and, with the assistance of Great Britain, eventually expelled the French from their country. Ferdinand was restored, but his treachery and his tyrannical proceedings excited the greatest dissatisfaction and indignation and led, in 1820, to a revolution of great importance, by which the constitution of the Cortes was restored. In 1823, with the help of a French army under the Duc d'Angoulême, Ferdinand was reinstated in his former authority. During this reign Spain lost the whole of her vast colonial empire on the continent of America.

In 1833, on the death of Ferdinand VII., the crown devolved by his will on his only child, Isabella II., and the Queen Mother, Christina, was appointed regent; whereupon Don Carlos, the late king's brother, laid claim to the crown, since when Spain has been involved in a succession of troubles from which she can only be said to have emerged within the last few years, since the accession of the present King Alfonso XII. It is now hoped that the country is once more on the road to progress. Great advances have undoubtedly been made, and nothing is wanted but peace and good government to assure the development of its great natural resources.

More extended information on this interesting subject must necessarily be sought in such works as those of Robertson, Prescott, Washington Irving, Dunham, Busk, &c., &c., as well as in the works of native original writers.

The following books, in addition to those already referred to, will be found both useful and interesting :—

Borrow's ' Bible in Spain.'

Hare's ' Wanderings in Spain.'

Baron Ch. Davillier's ' L'Espagne.'

And Germond de Lavigne's ' De l'Espagne et du Portugal' (one of the excellent *Guides Joanne* series).

The ' Guide Diamant,' an abridgment of the last mentioned work, will be found convenient for the pocket.

LIST OF THE PRINCIPAL OBJECTS OF INTEREST IN TOLEDO.

Cathedral.
Casa de Mesa.
Madre de Dios ó Palacio de los Abencerrajes.
San Juan de los Reyes.
Cláustro de idem.
Santa María la Blanca.
Tránsito.
Roca Tarpella.
Taller del Moro.
Alcázar.
Santa Cruz.
Puerta Malvardon.
Puerta del Sol.
Puerta Almadena y Visagra.
Mezquita del Cristo de la Luz.
Hospital de Tavera.
San Juan de la Penitencia.
Puente de San Martin.
Puente de Alcántara.
Baño de la Cava.
Santiago del Arrabal.
Fábrica de Armas.
Palacio de D. Pedro el Cruel.
Casa del Conde de Trastamara.
San Justo.
Santa Clara.
Casa del Rey Wamba.
Castillo de San Servando.
Palacio de Galiana.
Circo Romano.
Basílica de Santa Leocadia.
Various Moorish houses.

O

I will take this opportunity of mentioning—I ought perhaps to have done so before—that the crumbling piece of masonry known as the *Baño de la Cava*, or bath of Florinda, included in the above list, never could have been a bath at all at any period of the history of Toledo. There seems no reason to doubt that the old tower called by that name was one of the buttresses of a bridge which formerly crossed the Tagus at this point, and which was replaced by the bridge now bearing the name of San Martin, the older structure having been destroyed by a flood. This conclusion is fully borne out by the existence of similar ruins on the opposite bank of the river.

Whence then, it may be asked, arose the popular legend associated with this ruin, to which I have alluded in Chapter III. p. 42? Simply from the situation of the tower, which rises on the most picturesque part of the river, and precisely at the foot of the convent of San Agustin, the ancient palace of Don Rodrigo, from which the supposed *Baño* could be seen without any difficulty whatever. The chroniclers were anxious that the Gothic king, like David, should be enamoured in a bath of the lady whose frailty had caused such disaster to Spain, and they conceived the possibility of demonstrating by a series of incontrovertible arguments that this ruined buttress could be nothing less than a bath.

Thus arose the tradition, and thus do we gain no small insight into the process by which myths are manufactured. See the interesting 'Tradiciones de Toledo' by Señor Eugenio de Olavarria y Huarte, a welcome volume to all lovers of legendary lore.

A SPECIMEN OF BULL-RING SLANG.

TOROS.

CORRIDA 22ª DE ABONO.—17 DE OCTUBRE DE 1880.

A la hora é la funsion
y yoviendo á chaparron,
juimos á ver la corría.
¡ Qué diluviar! ¡ Si paesia
que estábamos en London !
    Como era güeno el carté,
chorreando jasta la pie
iban muchas criatura
á ver lidiá los seis Miura
á Angel, Curro y Rafaé.
    Metías entre cristale
toas las jembra juncale,
ni se asomaban siquiera ;
yo yovaba una á mi vera
de las mas menumentale.
    La acompañaba un peá
con su *castora* é timbá
y una espesie é surtú,
y sus chancla é cochú,
y su sombriya é percá.
    Un gachó de esos formale
de clase ministeriale,
limpio, gordo y relusiente,

O 2

dijo que era presiente
de un *clus* de los animale.

Y que iba por su parienta
que la funsion le revienta;
conque yo le ije que
quisiera ser un *chusqué*
sólo por la presienta.

Ayegando á la estasion,
bajamos del faeton
con agua jasta er cogote,
y nos pusieron un bote
dende ayí jasta er porton.

¡Si la afision será güena
toa la plasa estaba yena,
y er sol ni asomaba un ojo:
no jiso farta er despojo
pa dejar limpia la arena.

Toos cubierto con sombriya.
vimos salir las cuadriya
y al arguasí que Dios guarde;
y un *punto* gritó: ¡Qué tarde
pa lusir las pantorriya!

No hubo denguu mataor
que ijera al gobernaor
"que la tarde no se presta"
¿cómo premitió la fiesta
ese devino señor?

* *

Con que á una señal de D. Gabriel Lopez Dávila,
tiniente de servisio, salió el primer animar de punta, de

los sei de la vacá de D. Antonio Miura, vesino de Seviya, lusiendo la divisa verde y negra.

Nos santiguamo los unos á los otros, y colocados en sus puesto Manuel Gutierrez (Melones) y José Bayart (Badila), salió al estanque, que asina paesia el ruedo, *Cortijero*, colorao, meano, ancho de cuna, cornalon y astiblanco.

No tenia resentimiento con los cabayero, y escomensó reservao y sin desir sus pensamientos á naide, se juyó en cuanto que Melone le pinchó una ves y Badila otra.

Condenao á fuego intermitente, se pasaron argunos minutos jasta que se jayaron banderiyas con electrisiá.

—¿Quieren ostés mistos si es iguá?—preguntó un abonao con canalones, que estaba en un tendío, casi bramando contra la empresa hidráulica que nos largó ayer la corría.

Se jayaron á la fin los palos de música, y Gayo clavó un par cuarteando güeno, y un paliyo, despué de dos salías á toro corrío ; Juan Molina cumplió con un par de cairele cuarteando, traseritos y andándole serca ó la recámara el animal.

Rafael vestía de asur con oro. Jayó á la res tan retraida como salió y preocupá con asuntos de familia, reselando de los amigo ; y parando los piese y con saber, se tiró, *cuarteando*, á volapió, y resurtó una estocá corta y una mijita contraria, saliendo por piese de la cara der toro.

El diestro meresió las parmas qué le tocaron, por la brega.

Estando en pié el toro, escomensaron á tocar las trompeta pa el arrastre.

—No tiene na é particular—me ijo un vesino.—¿Ha oido usté desir que los reloje se trastornan con la humedá?

Pus lo mismo pasa con los estrumentos de música, que se adelantan con el agua.

***

And so on to the end of the chapter.

The uncomplimentary reflection, at the beginning, on the climate of the British Metropolis will not pass unnoticed.

INDEX.

A.

Alcalá de Henáres, 99.
Academia de San Fernando, 139.
Alhambra, 80.
Almodovar Castle, 64.
Antequera, 76.
Arroz a la Valenciana, 158.
Arragonese costume, 103.
Athenæum, article by Señor Riaño, 173–187.
Avignon, 110.

B.

Baile Nacional, a, 106.
Baño de la Cava, 194.
BARCELONA, 115; Cathedral, 116; Sta. Maria del Mar, 117; Plaza de la Constitucion, 117; Town Hall, 117; Post-office, 118; climate, 118.
Basque peasantry, 150.
Bayonne, 7.
Beds, 159.
Beggars, 13.
Biarritz, 7.
Bible, Polyglot Edition (Complutensian), 99.
' Biblioteca Universal,' 171–2.
Bidassoa (river), 154.
Brigands, 160–1.
Bull-fight at Madrid, 22.
Bull-ring slang, specimen of, 195.

Burgos, 9; *Fonda del Norte,* 9; streets, 9; *Plaza Mayor,* 10; the Cid, 10; Ximena, 10; Cathedral, 10; coffer of the Cid, 11; chapel of the Constable, 11; beggars, 13; street urchins, 13; St. Nicholas, 13; *Santa Gadea,* or *Agueda,* 13; *Cartuja de Miraflores,* 14; Castle, 15; *Arco de Sta. Maria,* 15; *Palacios,* 16.

C.

Cafés, 160.
Calatayud, 102.
Cervantes, birthplace (Alcalá), 100.
Châteaux en Espagne, 64.
Cid, the, 10; coffer of, 11; at Valencia, 137.
Circular tickets, 109.
Complutum of Romans, 99.
Cookery, 157.
Cordova, 54; *Fonda Suiza,* 54; Mosque, 55; Calahorra Tower, 57; Azzahra, Palace of (note), 58; Casino or Club, 59; *Patios,* 60–1.

D.

Dances, some Spanish national, 106.
Diligence, a journey by, 91.
Duval, Etablissements, or de Bouillon (Paris), 4.

E.

El Tribunal de las Aguas, at Valencia, 167.
Escorial, 17.
' L'Espagnol tel qu'on le parle,' 170.
Etablissements Duval, or de Bouillon, at Paris, 4.

F.

Ferrer, St. Vicente, his miracles for the conversion of the Jews, 67, 68.
Fontarabia, 151–3.

G.

Galiana, Palacio de, aud legend, 147.
Generalife, 85.
Gerona, 114.
Gonsalvo de Cordova, 77.
GRANADA, 75 ; *Fonda de los Siete Suelos,* 78 ; *Torre de los Siete Suelos,* 78 ; streets, 79 ; markets, 79 ; Cathedral, 79 ; *La Torre de Justicia,* 80 ; Generalife, 85 ; Cartuja, 88 ; *Alcaiceria,* 88 ; Birarambla, 89 ; Gipsies, 89.

H.

Halévy, 'Les Mousquetaires de la Reine,' 6, 7.
Hamilcar, 119.
Hannibal, 119, 130.
History of Spain, Summary of, 188.
Hotels, 156.
Hostalrich, 115.

I.

" Ile des Faisans," 154.
Irrigation, 166.
Irun, 8.
Irving, W. (ref.), viii.

J.

Jaen, 93.
Jativa, 138.
Juanes, 127.

L.

Laila and Manuel, 78.
Language, 169.
Living, cost of, 159.
Literature, 173–187.
List of Principal Objects of Interest in Toledo, 193.
Loja, 76.
Luz, St. Jean de, 8.

M.

MADRID, 18; Royal Picture Gallery, 18; *Puerta del Sol*, 19; public walks, 19; Spanish ladies, 20; *Teatro de Apollo*, 20; a *zarzuela*, 21; a bull-fight, 22; *Plaza de Toros*, 29; a Protestant service, 29; *Plaza Mayor*, 50; bull-feasts, 51; *Plaza Oriente*, 53; Philip III., statue of, 53; Philip IV., ditto, 53.
Marchena, 76.
Martorell, 118.
Montpellier, 113.
Musée Fabre, 113.

N.

Nimes, 112.

O.

Olla podrida, 158.
Orgaz, Count, picture of burial of, 145.

P.

Palacios, 16, 153.
Pasajes, 8.
Perpignan, 113.
Police, 160, 164.
Polyglot Bible, Ximenes' edition of the, 99.
Pont du Gard, 112.
Puchero, 158.

Q.

Quixote, Don, 1, 63.

R.

Railways, 156.
Riaño, Señor J. F., article by, 173–187.
Rock of the Lovers, 77.
Rivers, Lord, at Loja, 76.

S.

Saguntum, 130.
St. Jean de Luz, 8.
San Sebastian, 149, 150.

SEVILLE, 65; Hôtel de Madrid, 65; Murillo, 65; Zurbaran, 65; Cathedral, 66; Giralda Tower, 67; *Puerta del Perdon*, 67; Lonja, 68; Alcazar, 68; Pedro the Cruel, 68; gardens, 69; Maria Padilla, 70; promenades, 70; *Torre del Oro*, 70; Triana, 71; San Telmo (Palace), 71; *Alameda de Hercules*, 71; streets, 73; climate, 73; the Barber of Seville, 74.
Siguenza, 101.
'Statesman's Year Book' cited, 31.

T.

TARRAGONA, 119; Cathedral, 121; cloisters, 122; *San Pablo*, 123.
Ticknor's 'History of Spanish Literature' cited, 21; referred to, 171, 2.
TOLEDO, 32; Cathedral, 34; choir stalls, 35; *Retablo*, 36; Mozarabic chapel, 36; Alcazar, 40; *San Juan de los Reyes* and cloisters, 41; Roderick and Florinda, 42; Bridge of St. Martin, 43; *El Tránsito*, and *Sta. Maria la Blanca*, 44; Toledan Jews, 45; Hospital of *Santa Cruz*, 46; *Puerta del Sol* and de *Visagra*, 47; *Cristo de la Luz*, 142; *Casa de Mesa*, 143; *Taller del Moro*, 144; *San Pedro Martir*, 144; *San Tomé*, 145; Moorish steeples, 146; List of Principal Objects of Interest in, 193.
Travelling, 156.

U.

Universities, 102.

V.

VALENCIA, 124; *Mercado*, 125; *Lonja de Seda*, 126; Cathedral, 126; Juanes, 127; Museum, 127; walls and gates, 128; *Orchatas*, 130.
Venus Salambo, 66, 71, 72.

W.

Water, 164.
Wells (Moorish), 166.
Webster, Rev. Wentworth, book on Spain referred to, 102, 187.

X.

Ximenes, 99, 100.

Z.

ZARAGOZA, 104; Cathedral, 104; *Torre Nueva*, 105; market place, 105; a *Baile Nacional*, 106.

Zurbaran, 65.

LONDON: PRINTED BY EDWARD STANFORD, 55, CHARING CROSS, S.W.